THE HOSTAGE OF ZIR

In this far-reaching fantasy-adventure, L. Sprague de Camp continues his famed *Krishna* series: the future history of an Earth dominated by Brazil, and of an interstellar Empire in which Portuguese is the spacefaring language of the Galaxy.

Following THE QUEEN OF ZAMBA and THE TOWER OF ZANID, THE HOSTAGE OF ZIR returns to a far outpost of Empire, the planet Krishna—a wilderness of blue woods under three moons, where square-riggers sail the inland seas, where fierce humanoids with feathery antennae cross swords in endless war.

Krishna is a "reserve," where the warrior citizens of a medieval society are protected from technology by Interstellar Law. And in the complex, heroic and often humorous interplay between these warriors and the bureaucrats of Empire, de Camp creates the wonder and excitement that characterizes SF at its best!

L. SPRAGUE DE CAMP

THE HOSTAGE OF ZIR

A BERKLEY BOOK

published by

BERKLEY PUBLISHING CORPORATION

Berkley Publishing Corporation
200 Madison Avenue
New York, N.Y. 10016

SBN 425-03870-X

*BERKLEY MEDALLION BOOKS are published by
Berkley Publishing Corporation
200 Madison Avenue
New York, N.Y. 10016*

BERKLEY MEDALLION BOOK ® TM 757,375

Printed in the United States of America

Berkley Edition, NOVEMBER, 1978

CONTENTS

NOTE ON PRONUNCIATIONS

While the reader may render the exotic names in the story as he likes, the author's usage with Varasto names is as follows: *a* and *á* as in "add" and "wad" respectively; other vowels about as in Spanish. Among consonants, *k* and *q* as in "keep" and "quote" regardless of adjacent sounds; *gh* = French uvular *r*; *kh* = German *ch*; ' = a glottal stop or cough; others as in English. Words ending in a consonant or a diphthong are stressed on the last syllable; those ending in a simple vowel are usually but not always stressed on the next to the last. Hence Balhib is "bal-HEEB"; Hershid is "hair-SHEED"; Sadabao is "sad-ab-OW"; Sotaspé is "saw-TASS-peh"; and Tázád is "Tah-ZODD." Beizi rhymes with "lazy"; Ziro is "ZEE-raw"; Zirou, "zee-RO." Castanhoso, a common Portuguese name, is approximately (depending on the dialect) "kush-TAH-nyew-soo."

THE HOSTAGE OF ZIR

THE RELUCTANT SWORDSMAN

When the *Goyaz* touched down at Novorecife, the loudspeaker boomed: "*Chégamos; todos passageiros fora!* We have arrived; all passengers out!"

Airlocks hissed, doors clanged, and the passengers shuffled down the ramp. Terrans marveled at the spectacular cloud effects and the peculiar vegetation, with its leaves not only of green but also pink, blue, and purple. They eagerly sniffed the warm spring air of the planet's subtropical zone.

At the foot of the ramp, the fat security officer, Cristôvão Abreu, watched them come. The dozen tourists from the Magic Carpet Travel Agency, recognizable by their red arm bands, formed a block in the middle of the line. Abreu picked out their courier, Fergus Reith, who was flitting about like an agitated sheep dog, counting his charges and chivvying them to stay in line and close ranks. This pale, thin young man with carrot-red hair did not impress Abreu as quite the fearless leader. With the instinct of a longtime policeman, Abreu foresaw trouble with this group.

The twelve tourists and their guide soon stood at counters in the customs room. Under the direction of a big, scowling Russian, the customs officers went through their baggage.

Otto Schwerin, the stubby tourist with bad teeth and cameras hung all over him, had trouble. Some of his cameras were neither small enough to hide in the hand nor equipped with self-destruct mechanisms. After expostulating in voluble German and broken English, he had to leave them under seal.

Once through customs, the gaggle of tourists got red-carpet treatment. The *Comandante*, silver-haired William Desmond Kennedy, shook hands all around and introduced Security Officer Abreu, Comptroller Angioletti, and Magistrate Keshavachandra.

"You are celebrities," said Kennedy. "This is the first guided tour to reach Krishna. Earthmen are after coming here for decades, but they've mostly been scientists, adventurers, missionaries, and officials. This is the beginning of organized tourism."

"Then," asked Fergus Reith, "the Middle Kingdom Travel Bureau hasn't shown up yet?"

"They have not, sir. You're the first."

"That's something. There's been a race among the agencies to bring the first party to Krishna, and we thought the Chinese might have beaten us to it. We could hardly match the resources of that government. But you know, Mr. Kennedy, you're something of a celebrity yourself. The terran press calls you the most successful of all the terran administrators abroad."

"Do they now? That's very flattering. But you must remember, Mr.—ah—Reith, that back in the days of the British Empire, we Irish were very successful colonial administrators." Kennedy chuckled. "Having grown up in an atmosphere of hospitality, flattery, treachery, and murder, we weren't surprised when we encountered these things in the colonies."

A small, squirrel-like man came in. Kennedy said, "Let me present Senhor Herculeu Castanhoso, assistant to Senhor Abreu. He'll get you outfitted."

Castanhoso took the party to their quarters. When Reith tried out his Portuguese on Castanhoso, the latter laughed.

"Que está cômico, o Senhor Dom Herculeu?" asked Reith.

"Excuse me," said Castanhoso, "but I was marveling at your European pronunciation."

"Well, the fellow who made the phonograph records I studied from spoke European Portuguese."

"Bem. Our Brazilian form, which we use in the Viagens Interplanetarias, is closer to the Spanish. Now suppose I meet you all in front of the Compound in one hour, to take you to the outfitting shop."

The outfitter was the first Krishnan whom Reith had seen at close range. He was about the size and shape of a tall, lean earthman—taller than Reith, who was of good height himself. The Krishnan's skin had a faint olive-green tinge and his hair a dark, bluish-green sheen. His features were not unlike those of Reith's tourists—all but one of them Caucasoids—but flatter and more oriental-looking.

When Reith looked closely, he picked out many small differences: the pointed ears, the form of the teeth, and so on. The most conspicuous feature was the Krishnan's external organs of smell: a pair of feathery appendages, like a moth's antennae. They sprouted up and out from the inner ends of the Krishnan's eyebrows, like a pair of extra brows.

Castanhoso explained: "Years ago, earthmen went out disguised with wigs and dyes. It was not safe to travel otherwise. Now we have normal relations with nearby states, and their people know we are not all scoundrels or sorcerers. Likewise, they are no longer so easily fooled; most of them know a terran voice. For the more distant parts, however, we still advise the old disguises. Now I present Mr. Sivird bad-Fatehán, our outfitter."

The Krishnan said: "May ze stars favor you. Ze Senhor Dom Herculeu and I, we have already discuss your requirements. You will need some rough clozes for ze outdoors, and formal costumes for presentation at ze court of Dur...."

Because of lack of space, the tourists had brought few changes of clothes. For most sightseeing, terran garments would do; but it was thought that, for the court of Dur, it were better to follow local custom.

"Is this one of those courts," said Sylvester Pride, "where the dames go around with bare tits? Boy, I can't wait to see that!"

"You are mistaken, Mr. Pride," said Castanhoso coldly. "That is the custom at Rosid and Hershid, but Baianch is nearly a thousand kilometers north of here. I must warn all of you that you will need to dress more warmly. It is like going from your Philadelphia to—to—what would be an example, Mr. Reith?"

Reith thought. "Montreal."

For formal outfits, most of the party chose sober costumes. But the two tanned, muscular young men, Considine and Turner, who jingled with jewelry and kept to themselves, would out-peacock the peacock. The handsome Venezuelan couple named Guzmán-Vidal also chose colorful garb. Valerie Mulroy, a tall, angular, but good-looking woman, wanted a bare-breasted gown. It took the combined efforts of Sivird and Castanhoso to dissuade her. Reith was relieved; as he had reason to know, her assets were modest.

Next morning, Castanhoso greeted Reith: *"Bom*

dia, Senhor Dom Fergus! Como vai?"

"Bem, obrigado. E o Senhor?"

"Good! Now I take you to the *ginásio*, where you will be trained."

"How about my tourists?"

"We have some little local tours planned, to keep them happy while you enjoy the ministrations of the Senhor Heggstad."

In the gym, Reith found a stocky, bald, blue-eyed, burly man flinging himself about on the parallel bars.

"Senhor Dom Fergus," said Castanhoso, "this is Ivar Heggstad, in charge of physical survival. *Até logo!"*

"How do you do, Mr. Haystack?" said Reith.

Heggstad felt Reith's biceps. "*Uff!* Too skinny. How do you expect to survive in a vorld where everything is depending on the physical?"

"Please! I didn't ask for this job, but now I've got to make the best of it."

"You are not a regular tourist guide?"

"No sir! I was assistant office manager at Magic Carpet, in Philadelphia. The courier assigned to this tour got married. Naturally, his bride wouldn't stand for his going off for a quarter-century, objective time. That's why people who make these trips are nearly always without close family ties on earth: the difference between objective and subjective time. His back-up man was in the hospital, and all our other regular couriers were out on tour, or pregnant, or something. We couldn't find a free-lance guide to take over; so, being single without close kin, I was drafted."

"They couldn't have made you go. You could have quit your yob, unless America has changed."

"I know. I suppose I didn't fight very hard because in all the science-fiction novels I read as a kid, the hero goes to some distant planet, has thrilling adventures, and marries a beautiful native princess. One fellow,

5

Otis Burroughs or some such name, wrote a lot of stories like that.... But none of these old romancers tells about the practical difficulties."

"Who vants to read a story about practical difficulties? Vell, have you had *any* guiding experience?"

"Some local guiding around historic Philadelphia, and one little Latin American tour. That didn't turn out very well. One couple got lost in Bogotá and weren't found for days. Another man, taking a picture at Machu Picchu, backed off a cliff and was killed."

"Those things happen. But let us get to business. Do you ride? Sail? Fence? Shoot the bow? Have you had military experience?"

Reith shook his head. "None of these things. If somebody had told me a year ago that I'd need these medieval skills, I might have done something about it. As it is, I'm just an ex-schoolteacher and office manager—a paper-shuffler—who plays a little golf and was put here by happenstance."

Heggstad sighed. "Ah, vell, in a year I could maybe make a real man of you. In a mere fifteen days—but ve shall see. Firsht, see how many times you can chin yourshelf on that bar."

Later, Reith sat in the Nova Iorque Bar, trying out kvad, the local tipple. With him was Castanhoso. Reith groaned. "After a day with that Norse physical-culture fanatic, I haven't been so stiff and sore in my life."

"*Sinto muito.* But I, too, have had troubles. That Schwerin! Every time it is time to go, he is off somewhere, taking one more photo. And I think the Senhora Mulroy would strike up an intrigue with any big Krishnan male she sees, if she could get him alone for ten minutes."

"That nympho!" said Reith. "She kept us busy on the *Goyaz.* First me—an education, you might say.

6

Then we quarreled when I stopped her from smoking a cigarette. So she took up with Afonso, the steward. Maybe you noticed Afonso looking a little pale and wan."

"Yes, I suppose that little old professor, her husband, is no longer able to keep her stoked."

"She's got the money."

"*Entendido*. But does he tolerate these games?"

"He seems to turn a blind eye, as we say. I guess he needs all the help he can get in that department."

Castanhoso shrugged. "Tell me about the others."

"Well, the middle-aged black woman is Miss Shirley Waterford, a retired schoolteacher who inherited money."

"She seems nice, except when she wants to argue with everybody about racism. Go on."

"The stout French couple are Aimé and Mélanie Jussac; he's a retired jeweler. The two young men in extreme clothes—the dear boys, Valerie calls them—are Maurice Considine and John Turner. The big, muscular one is Considine; the shorter, plumper one is Turner. They're *that* way." Reith flipped a limp wrist. "Turner hasn't given any trouble, but Considine is always complaining. He's a sculptor or something; throws his weight around and likes his bottle. Turner seems to have the money.

"The real old lady is Mrs. Whitney Scott. She could buy all the rest of us. Be careful with her; she's well over two hundred and fragile. That clown who wears funny hats and tells bad jokes is Sylvester Pride—"

An uproar arose outside. When Reith and Castanhoso got out, Santiago Guzmán-Vidal was chasing his wife with a knife. Reith tripped him, and Castanhoso jumped on his back. Between them, they got the knife away from him. He sputtered:

"I kill them both! She was making eyes at that big Russian *matón*—"

Pilar Guzmán came back when she saw it was safe. Santiago Guzmán sank to his knees in front of her, crying:

"Kill me! ¡*Lo merezco!*"

"¡*Ah, queridisimo!*" she said, folding him in her arms. They had a passionate reconciliation, with tears and kisses, until Guzmán suggested that they go back to their quarters.

"*Un momento,*" she said, and departed. Guzmán looked dreamily after her.

"After the esstorm, the sunshine," he said.

Castanhoso asked: "Do you do this sort of thing often?"

"Bery often! All the time, in fact!"

"It sounds strenuous, Senhor."

"It is the esspice of life. And now my adored one awaits. ¡*Arriba!*" Off went Guzmán-Vidal.

"Whew," said Castanhoso. "Did you have that, too?"

"Oh, yes," said Reith. "One time Santiago hid in my cabin when his wife was looking for him to brain him with a camera tripod. Valerie Mulroy had made passes at him, and he didn't discourage her. If that's married life, I'm glad I'm single."

"In your business you practically have to be, because of the time lag. How do you make that ass Pride shut up?"

"Short of hitting him with a club, I don't know. There's at least one in every group." Reith yawned. "Now I have to eat with my lambs. Then I'm supposed to study a couple of your foul Krishnan languages, but I'm so tired I'll probably fall asleep in the first declension."

"Gozashtandou and Durou are not too hard. They are as much alike as, say, Spanish is like Portuguese, and they have fewer irregularities than most European tongues. Katai-Jhogorai is something else; it belongs to another language family."

"We're to depend on Prince Tashian's man as interpreter there."

"Watch yourself; I mistrust that Tashian."

"What's the matter with him?" asked Reith.

"I do not know. It is just a feeling. In police work, we tend to get suspicious of everybody."

"Where are you taking them tomorrow?"

"Through the Hamda'. They can unload some of their ill-gotten wealth on the vendors of trinkets, all of whom are salivating in anticipation. Krishnans think all Terrans as rich as Dezful the pirate king."

"They have to be pretty well fixed to make the trip," said Reith, yawning again. "*Boa noite.*"

Ivar Heggstad said: "So what if you are stiff? A little vorkout vill soon fix that. Come on, now: deep knee bends. Down! Up! Down!..."

When Reith thought himself on the verge of collapse, Heggstad produced an armful of fencing masks and padding. "Put these on. Now take this."

He handed Reith a fencing saber with a blunt point and a big bowl-shaped guard. Reith looked dubious, saying:

"In the stories, the hero goes to work with a skinny little épée and skewers the villains while they're waving big cutting swords around."

"*Akk ja!* Those little toothpicks are all right for a couple of yentlemen in silk breeches and powdered vigs, on level ground vit seconds to see everything is done by the rules. Here, the Terran comes up against a Krishnan in armor, and his blade bends double. Or the Krishnan hits his blade real hard and snaps it. Then the gallant earthman is dead. So, for these conditions, nineteenth-century saber is the thing. *En garde!*"

9

Reith ended the day with his right arm black and blue to the shoulder, where Heggstad had whacked him. He joined his tourists on their return from the Hamda'. This was a suburb of Novorecife outside the wall. The dwellers were a raffish lot of deracinated Krishnans and broken-down Terran adventurers. There one could buy native artifacts, gimcrack souvenirs, and real or fake antiquities.

Old Mrs. Scott had bought a pair of earrings allegedly worn by the pirate Dezful. Turner came back festooned with a necklace said to have been worn by Dángi when she was imprisoned in the haunted tower. Considine and Pride each got a sword supposed to have belonged to the hero Qarar. When Reith spoke to Aimé Jussac, the portly jeweller smiled indulgently.

"They tried all sorts of junk on me," he said. "Me, I played dumb. The dumber I played, the more fantastic the stories they told about their little pieces of jewelry. Then Castanhoso let slip that I was the retired vice-president of Tiffany and Company. *Zut!* You should have seen their faces. But then we settled down to a plain business talk, with the little Hercules interpreting. I picked up a piece not bad, at a good price."

Jussac showed a fire-opal ring. "Of course," he continued, "the art of faceting is in its infancy here. I could show them a thing or two, if that Saint-Rémy treatment did not tie the tongue whenever an earthman tries to give a Krishnan technical information. In passing," he added with a shrewd look, "do you get a commission from local merchants to whom you steer your tourists, the way guides do on earth?"

"No," said Reith. "For that, you have to live in the place. At Magic Carpet, we disapprove of such commissions. We can't control the local guides, but we bear down on couriers from the home base."

• • •

During the following days, when not straining his guts in Heggstad's gymnasium, or being lashed and prodded with a fencing saber, or cracking his skull over the Gozashtando and Duro tongues, Fergus Reith learned to ride. He rode an aya, which had six legs, horns, a hard trot, and a mean disposition. He also rode a shomal, which had only four legs, looked something like a humpless camel, and tended to balk like a mule. He learned to use Krishnan eating tools, which were little spears held like chopsticks.

Although Reith felt like a heretic on the losing side of a theological argument with the Chief Inquisitor, he tried not to complain. His ancestor Robert the Bruce, he told himself, had not complained in equally dire straits.

While Reith was being hardened for his task, Castanhoso took Reith's tourists up the Pichidé River to Rimbid and down the river to Qou. At Qou they saw a village of the tame Koloftuma—the tailed primitives of Krishna. The sight touched off a furious argument between Professor Winston Mulroy and Shirley Waterford.

"They were still at it when I left them," Castanhoso told Reith. "Mulroy brought in intelligence tests, inter-species fertility, and those fossil terran ape-men called austral-something. The Senhorita Waterford just talked louder and louder about his racism. Anyway, nobody got lost or hurt."

One of Reith's last conferences before leaving was with Pierce Angioletti, the Comptroller. Angioletti was a thin-lipped, graying, reserved man with a Bostonian twang. After they had gone over maps, written accounts of the lands the party was to see, and the expedition's financial accounts, Angioletti said:

"I can't tell you too often to be careful. Between us, I opposed letting a mob of tourists loose on Krishna yet."

"Too risky, you think?"

"Just so. We have enough trouble when the people we've been getting—missionaries, scientists, and adventurers—go off and disappear. The I.C. insists we avoid anything smacking of imperialism, while the terran governments give us a hard time when we can't find out what happened to their citizens, let alone rescue them. The French even put pressure on us when that fellow Borel vanished in Dur, although everyone knew he was just a con man."

"What did happen to him? After all, we're going to Dur."

Angioletti shrugged. "If I knew, there wouldn't be any mystery. But God knows what'll happen when you set out with a dozen *Ertsuma*, some of them obvious damned fools. If nobody gets murdered or seized for ransom, I'll eat my codfish with chocolate sauce."

Reith sighed. "I can only do my best. What did Castanhoso mean, warning me against the Regent Tashian? Could he have had anything to do with Borel's disappearance?"

"I don't know. Tashian's a shrewd operator with no more scruples than you expect of a Renaissance prince. But it's to his advantage to build up tourist traffic to Dur, so he'll probably stand by his promises.

"I don't think he did Borel in. Felix Borel disappeared in one of the wilder parts, not under the government's control. The kind of man he was, he had it coming to him sooner or later. He tried one of his con games on that Russian big shot, Trofimov. But he picked the wrong sucker. Trofimov caught on and might have had Borel jailed, or perhaps quietly murdered, if Borel hadn't skedaddled.

12

"Mr. Reith, just imagine you're Thomas Cook, but living in, say, the eighteenth century. You're taking a party of Europeans on a tour of North America, visiting the most warlike tribes, like the Iroquois and the Blackfeet. That gives you an idea."

"You sure fill me with confidence," said Reith.

"Oh, don't let it worry you. If you get into trouble in Majbur, go see Gorbovast, the Gozashtando commissioner. He does some chores for us, and he can fix anything."

Later, on one of the paths of the compound, Reith fell into talk with Magistrate Keshavachandra. The judge was a slight, brown-skinned man, shorter than Reith, with bushy gray eyebrows and a fringe of gray hair around his bald head.

"Judge," said Reith, "I'm discouraged. I must have done something pretty awful in a previous incarnation to be put in this fix."

"How so?"

"I'm not an experienced tourist guide; yet, circumstances have dumped me into a situation where I need to be Hercules, d'Artagnan, and Talleyrand, all at once. But I'm not. Heggstad has been training me physically, but it would take years to make me into the kind of muscle man he is. I've been practicing Durou and Gozashtandou with some help from Sivird. But all I can say is a few simple things like 'Pour me a drink' and 'Where is the toilet?' It's one thing to say 'Two fried eggs, please,' in a foreign language, but quite another to carry on an intelligent conversation. I have just the merest smattering of all the things I'm supposed to know, and no time to master any of them.

"I feel doomed; but we've taken these yucks' money, so it's up to me to give them their tour if it kills me."

Keshavachandra asked: "Are you familiar with the

Bhagavad Gîtâ, Mr. Reith?"

Reith looked puzzled. "No. That's some Hindu legend, isn't it?"

"It's much more than that. Let me explain. The *Bhagavad Gîtâ* is a section of the *Mahâbhârata*, the old Indian epic, sometimes called the world's longest poem. As a scientific materialist, I don't believe the legends; but like your Bible it has some useful philosophy.

"The *Bhagavad Gîtâ* tells how Prince Arjuna is about to fight in a great battle between the Pandavas and the Kauravas. Arjuna's charioteer is Krishna, an incarnation of God. Arjuna gets qualms about fighting against some of his own kinsmen. But Krishna tells him that, since God has made him a warrior, his job is to be the best warrior he can and not to worry about who gets killed.

"So, young man, let me be your Krishna. You find yourself in a fix for which you are not prepared. Well, make yourself prepared. What you don't know, learn. Practice your exercises and your languages every spare minute, and you may find that you do better than you think possible."

Reith went to the gym, to find Heggstad practicing tumbling. "Ivar," he said, "I'd like to borrow some of that fencing stuff to take on the tour. A couple of those jackets and masks—"

"Hey!" said Heggstad. "Not my good fencing sabersh! I couldn't replace them. Here, you can have these."

The gymnast produced a pair of singlesticks, the thickness of broom handles, with bowl-shaped wicker guards. "Have you got a real sword for yourself?"

"No. Was I supposed to?"

"How much good you think one of those sticks would do you against a real blade? Sivird can sell you

14

one at a fair price. Not so pretty as you get in the Hamda', but good steel."

"I can charge it to the tourist agency. How do I keep it from getting tangled up in my legs?"

"Vear it high and hold the scabbard when you come to stairsh and such-like. Don't vear it around native taverns, or some drunken tough guy may pick a fight; but you get more respectable treatment from ordinary Krishnans when you vear vun. Who you going to fence vit? Poor old Mrs. Scott?"

Reith smiled. "Maybe I can con Mr. Pride into a match. One good whack at his fat butt would be worth the trip."

II.

RIVER-BOAT FOLLIES

The priest whom Regent Tashian was sending as guide and interpreter was supposed to arrive on the tenth of Khástin. When he failed to appear, some of the tourists grumbled. Santiago Guzmán-Vidal shrugged, saying:

"What do you expect of these half-barbarous people? They have no sense of time."

Fergus Reith looked hard at Guzmán-Vidal, who was late for everything. Reith spent the extra time grimly working at his new skills. When, after a session with Heggstad, he emerged panting from the gym, Valerie Mulroy asked:

"Do you really like that sort of thing, Fearless?" To his tourists, Reith had become "Fearless Leader" or simply "Fearless."

"No, I hate it."

"Then why do it?"

"Because I hate worse being caught with my pants down."

She gave him a look that in a man would have been called a leer. "I could make a dirty crack about that. But you're over-conscientious; you take life too hard. Take things as they come, the way I do."

"Easy for you to say, Valerie. You don't have the respon—"

"Fergus!" bellowed Heggstad, "Get back in here! You got to learn to nail your man when he parries in *seconde*!"

When Reith had returned and resumed his mask, Heggstad went on: "On earth, ve have learned better. Ve parry low-right in octave, so ve don't vaste time turning the hand back to supine. That fraction of a second can make all the difference. Now, you lunge, low and to your left. When I parry in *seconde*, double and kill me!"

Before Reith could obey, Castanhoso's voice called: "Senhor Reith! Come quickly! I think your man is arriving!"

Still wearing his fencing jacket, Reith followed the security officer down through the river gate and out on the pier. Across the river, small in the distance, he saw a barge being towed upstream by a team of shaihans.

The animals plodded up the tow path to a point across the river, where another small pier led out from the shore. The crew tied up, unhitched the team, and took them aboard the vessel. They set out under oars and a triangular sail across the current to the north side.

As the Krishnans tied up at the Novorecife pier, a Krishnan in a long robe stepped ashore. After him came two servants carrying baggage. Castanhoso accosted the man:

"The Senhor is Khorsh baf-Ferzao?"

"That is so," said the man in good Portuguese. "Bless you, my sons."

"Thank you," said Castanhoso. When he had introduced Reith, he added: "We expected you several days ago."

"What is one day more or less in eternity?" replied Khorsh. "I was detained in Majbur on sacerdotal business."

Next day, Reith's tourist party, together with several other passengers, boarded the *Zaidun* for the return to Majbur. The shaihans remained in their shipboard stall, for they were used on upstream journeys only. Going downstream, the current and sail sufficed.

When Reith had counted his tourists and their pieces of baggage twice and had thrice checked through his papers to be sure of all the maps, letters of introduction, and other documents, the crew pushed out from the pier. They rowed to the middle of the stream, where the current ran most swiftly. Thereafter, one man at the tiller and two more on oars sufficed to keep the craft in midstream.

Captain Ozum said to Reith, in broken Portuguese: "Ship all cleaned up, specially you-for. You like?"

"*Estupendo*," said Reith. Although there had been some scrubbing, the vessel still stank of the shaihans and of the cargo carried on previous voyages. Since the shaihans were in the stern and the passengers in the bow, and since the prevailing wind was from the west, there was no escaping the draft beasts' aroma.

They sailed eastward, paralleling the massive concrete wall that ran along the riverside to protect Novorecife. The pier and the boathouse were soon out of sight.

The terrain along the south bank flattened out, until

there was nought to see between river and sky save a dark-green strip of tall reeds, with a scattering of exotic-looking multicolored trees. Flying creatures on brown, leathery wings rose, squawking and honking and whistling, from the reeds. They circled and flapped away.

The reeds gave way to low brown bluffs. A sloping green area, littered with large, regular-looking stones, came in sight.

"That is a ruined city," said Khorsh, while Reith translated. "Nobody knows who built it or when. It is locally called Saba-o-Astiremá, which means merely 'place of stones.' Could these stones speak, who knows what tales they might tell?"

They neared Qou on the south bank. Reith asked: "Does anyone want to stop here? It's on our itinerary; but we're behind schedule, and you've already seen it with Castanhoso."

"I want to," said Shirley Waterford. "I'm going to give that official a piece of my mind, about the slavery and the discrimination against the tailed Krishnans—"

"Oh, no, you're not!" said Reith. "We run enough risks without stirring up more alligators. You can look. You can even take pictures if you're discreet. But you're not to say a word against local customs or beliefs." He added in Gozashtandou: "Steady as you go, Captain Ozum. We shall not stop."

"Squalid little place," said Considine. "Hardly like one of the cities Dunsany saw along the Yann."

Reith said: "So long as you're wearing that sword, Maurice, how about a little practice in using it?"

Soon they were cutting and thrusting with the singlesticks. Although he looked twice as muscular as Reith, Considine was the first to admit fatigue.

"You've been touring and taking it easy while I was working out in Heggstad's gym," said Reith.

Considine peeled off his white protective jacket and

mopped his streaming forehead. "How about a swim, Fearless? We could easily keep up with the boat."

Reith asked Khorsh. The priest threw up his hands. "Nay, my son, broach not such a thought! Know that in these waters dwells a creature called the *avval*, which could seize and devour you in a trice. And how should we replace so valiant a youth?"

"That's right; I remember reading about it." Reith turned to his party. "They have here a kind of cross between a crocodile and a junior sea serpent. So we'd better not. Professor Mulroy, how would you like to tell us about the local fauna and flora?"

On his South American tour, Reith had learned that, to keep his charges out of mischief, it was well to arrange some event for them whenever they had a long, inactive period. The elderly paleontologist was soon in full form:

"... you see, vertebrate evolution on Krishna has followed a course in many ways parallel to but also quite distinct from that on earth. Whereas on earth, one group of fishes, the Crossopterygii, made the transition from water to land, on Krishna two groups did it: the Tetrapoda, which have remained oviparous although they include the hominoid species, and the Hexapoda, who early developed viviparity."

"Why was that?" asked Mrs. Whitney Scott, who missed little.

"Probably a result of the fact that on earth, the continents are islands surrounded by a worldwide ocean, whereas on Krishna the seas are lakes surrounded by one worldwide land mass. So the transition from water to land was made twice independently. We have an earthly parallel, in the Periphthalmidae—"

"The what?" said Considine.

"A family of semiterrestrial gobies, called mud skippers, from Southeast Asia. They have begun the

transition to life on land. On the other hand, Krishnan
land vertebrates do not show the sharp distinctions
among Amphibia, Reptilia, and Mammalia that we are
accustomed to. Homoiothermism—warm-blooded-
ness, I suppose I should say—evolved early in both
taxa—"

"How about birds?" asked Shirley Waterford.

"It is like the snakes of Ireland: there are none.
Krishnan life has never developed the feather, so the
flying organisms are more comparable to our bats and
pterosaurs than to the class Aves. Now, as we ascend
the evolutionary scale—"

"Excuse me, Professor," said a pudgy brown
passenger, one of the several who did not belong to
Reith's party. "You seem to accept the false theory,
that all these evidences for evolution, on earth and
other planets, testify to actual events."

"Well?" snapped Mulroy.

"We servants of the Lords of Light know that truth
is different. Divine revelation proves that all those
fossil bones and things were put in the ground by the
Lords of Darkness—what you would call the Devil—
to seduce men away from the truth of God's crea-
tion—"

"You are, sir—?" said Mulroy.

"Excuse me; I am Ganesh Kosambi of Bombay,
humble representative of Board of Missions of the
Church of the Lords of Light—"

Reith interrupted: "Mr. Kosambi, please let
Professor Mulroy finish his lecture. We have plenty of
time between here and Majbur. If you want to preach
this afternoon, I'm sure we'd be glad to hear you."

Kosambi subsided. When afternoon arrived, those
not sleeping gathered in the bow to hear the
missionary. Kosambi told how his sect was founded by
Tallal Homsi, a Syrian whom God had directed to dig
up a book in unknown writing on sheets of electrum.

God also furnished him with a pair of miraculous spectacles. These enabled Tallal Homsi—before he was martyred by his Muslim fellow villagers—to read and transcribe the contents of the wonderful book. The book explained how God had sent out the Lords of Light, otherwise angels, to all habitable planets, bearing the seeds of living things of all kinds. . . .

Sylvester Pride turned away, remarking loudly: "Haw, what a lot of bullshit!"

Kosambi looked pained but carried on. Reith privately agreed about Kosambi's theology but would not have hurt the earnest little man's feelings.

Next morning, the *Zaidun* reached Gadri, larger than Qou but no metropolis. Reith told his people:

"There's not much to see here except the market and one temple. The things for sale are mostly staples and everyday working artifacts—no tourist gimcracks. The people haven't yet become attuned to tourism, but give 'em time. In any case, I advise you not to load yourselves down with junk this early. You'll have plenty of chances later."

They tramped from the waterfront to the main square, a few blocks away. Every time they stopped to look at something, curious Krishnans gathered around to stare. These temporary crowds grew until Reith felt apprehensive. While the Krishnans seemed good-natured, anything might happen if some trivial mischance touched off a disturbance.

At the temple, a plainly massive structure of rust-red sandstone, Khorsh, the Duro priest, spoke to the doorkeeper and then told Reith it would be all right to enter. Of course, a free-will offering in the collection box would be appreciated.

Inside, the gilded statue of the god sat cross-legged on its dais at the far end. The feeble flames of the lamps were reflected from the statue's gilt and the black wall of polished black onyx. Since the idol had four legs, its pose meant a complicated tangle of limbs. It also bore eight arms.

"It looks a little like Shiva," said Kosambi, who had tagged along. Reith was hardened to free-loaders who attached themselves to tour groups.

"It looks like a centipede to me," said Pride loudly. "Boy, couldn't he dance a jig, with all those legs? Like this." Pride began to demonstrate, hopping grotesquely in his shorts with his potbelly bouncing.

"Stop it, you damned fool!" hissed Reith.

"What? Who?" said Pride. "Look here, squirt—"

"If he doesn't stop you, I will!" said Mrs. Whitney Scott. The old lady limped forward, gripping her walking stick like a club.

"Oh, all right," mumbled Pride. "I didn't mean any harm."

Outside, they toured the market, where Pride insisted on buying and wearing a hat resembling a pink terran lampshade. They viewed an undistinguished little municipal hall and started back towards the pier. Turner said:

"Hey, Fearless! Maurice and I want to stop off for a drink. That's a place that sells 'em, isn't it?" He pointed to a tavern.

"I don't like to let the party split up—" said Reith.

"Oh, come on. We know the way back. If you take the others to the boat and get worried, you can come back here for us."

"All right," said Reith. Then the Mulroys and the Jussacs decided to stop for a drink, too.

"Only," said Jussac, "you will have to order and pay for us, since we don't speak the language."

Reith entered the tavern with the six drinkers and found a table. "Reverend Khorsh, will you please stay with them and order for them?"

"A strange request, my son, to me who drinks not.

24

But for your sake I will do it. Who knows what unlooked-for wisdom I may acquire thereby?"

"Thanks. Remember, the rest of you, come straight back to the boat when you finish."

When he went out to lead the remaining half of his gaggle back, Reith found that Schwerin had disappeared. After a frantic search, he found the man perched on the corner of a roof, photographing the square. The usual crowd of curious Krishnans had gathered below him, staring up.

As Reith fumed, a fragment of his rusty German returned. "*Herr Schwerin!*" he shouted. "*Bitte, kommen Sie herunter, sofort!*"

Schwerin gave a vague wave and smile and continued his photography. Reith took the remaining five back to the *Zaidun*.

He was about to return to gather up the rest of his group when a disturbance drew his attention. Maurice Considine appeared running, his empty scabbard slapping against his legs. After him came a big Krishnan waving a sword.

Considine pounded out on the pier and leaped aboard the *Zaidun*. So did the Krishnan. The other passengers scattered with cries of alarm, falling over one another to get out of the way.

Reith looked about for something to stop the pursuer. His eye lighted upon a pile of fencing equipment against the bulwark. He and Guzmán-Vidal had placed it there after a practice bout that morning. He snatched up one of the singlesticks.

As Considine ran past him, Reith stepped into the path of the Krishnan. He wanted to order the man to stop but could not think of the right words. He shouted: "Stop! *Halte-là! Páre!*" in hope that his tone would convey his meaning.

The Krishnan kept on, shouting "*Baghan!*" and swinging up his sword. Reith parried and felt the steel blade bite into the wood. There was a quick exchange of cuts and thrusts.

Reith lunged, aiming low and to his left. The Krishnan brought his blade around in a whistling parry in *seconde*. If it had landed, it might have severed the singlestick.

Remembering what Heggstad had pounded into him, Reith doubled and thrust. The point of the Krishnan's sword scarred the deck planks as Reith's blunt wooden point took the Krishnan in the chest. Reith put all his strength into the push.

As the two had circled, the Krishnan had come to stand with his back to the gunwale. Hence, as Reith pushed him, he backed into the low bulwark and fell over backwards. Splash!

Reith stepped after the Krishnan and looked down. The Krishnan's head emerged from the brown water with a strangled yell.

"He says 'Help!'" said Ganesh Kosambi, who had appeared beside Reith. "He cannot swim."

"Serve him right if he drowns," said Reith.

"You had better pull him out," said the missionary. "Otherwise there will be complications. You may find yourself in the Gadri jail. It is not a nice place."

Reith sighed. "I suppose you're right, damn it. Captain Ozum! Have you—what the devil's the word for 'rope'?"

The Krishnan, who had lost his sword, was pulled out. Reith said to Kosambi: "Tell him, please, that I don't know what started it, but I can't have people carving up my tourists."

Kosambi spoke. The Krishnan spat at Reith's feet and stalked off, just as the remaining tourists straggled back to the ship.

Now that it was over, Reith suddenly realized how close he had come to being killed. His knees sagged, and for an instant he thought he was going to faint. He grasped the gunwale to steady himself as his tourists flocked around. They drenched him with praise:

"Fearless, you were wonderful!" "He really is fearless, isn't he?" "A real swashbuckler!"

Reith managed a wan smile.

When the crowd had dispersed, Aimé Jussac confided to Reith: "I saw it. The Mr. Turner got to talking to Valerie Mulroy. You know, she would try even him, and she made her intentions evident. So Considine, jealous I suppose, made a—what you call a pass at this Krishnan, who was minding his own business at the next table. They had six or seven words of Portuguese in common, but—*chouette!*—it was enough."

That evening, when they were again out in mid-river, Reith got Considine aside and asked for his side of the story. Considine professed ignorance of the cause of the disturbance.

"Sure you didn't try—ah—undue familiarity with him?" asked Reith.

"I did not!" retorted Considine, drawing himself up. "I know what you mean. Look here, just because I have my own sexual preferences doesn't mean I'm some cruising queen. One more crack like that and I'll—"

"Okay, have it your own way. Just don't do it again, see? Did you lose your sword there?"

"Yeah. When he drew on me, I drew, too, but he knocked it out of my hand. Too bad; it belonged to that hero, what's-his-name."

Reith smiled. "My dear Maurice, if Qarar had really owned half the swords attributed to him, he'd have needed one of those Krishnan elephants called bishtars to carry them. You can buy as many as you like in Majbur, all just as authentic."

27

III.

THE EMERALD IDOL

On the right, along the low shores of the Pichidé estuary, the piers and wharves of the Free City of Majbur came into view. About these landing places clustered a swarm of local and river craft. There were fishing smacks, river barges, timber rafts, pleasure yachts, ferries, and water taxis. Beyond these, around the curve of the shore, rose a spiky fence of the masts and yards of deep-water ships. Here lay high-sided square-riggers from the stormy Va'andao Sea and lateeners with slanting yards from the more southerly ports. Here, too, were war galleys with bronzen beaks and gilded sterns, gleaming in the ruddy afternoon light of Roqir, under a greenish sky.

With much shouting of threats and curses towards other ships, Captain Ozum worked the *Zaidun* under oar power towards a berth. Reith asked:

"Father Khorsh, they sound as if they were going to riot. Is there any danger?"

"No, my son. They are always noisy, but rarely does anything come of it."

Reith consulted his notebook. "I'm supposed to get them to Haftid's Inn, at Forty-six Shodsir. Where would that street be?"

"Shodsir is not a street."

"*O que?* What is it, then?"

"O my son, have they not told you of the system of addresses used here? Shodsir is a block, and Forty-six is the forty-sixth building in that block."

"The forty-sixth counting from where?"

"Not the forty-sixth in any geographical sense, but the forty-sixth in order of construction."

Reith digested this concept. "Well, suppose I want to meet a fellow on a given street. Where do I tell him to go?"

"Streets in Majbur have no names. If you wished to meet your man on the street bounding the Shodsir on the north, you would say, Shodsir North. It is simple."

"To you, maybe. Then how do I find the Shodsir block?"

"Any hackney driver or litter bearer can take you thither."

"*Bem.* How shall I find these drivers and bearers? We shall also need porters."

Khorsh smiled. "Fear not, my son. The gods will provide."

Reith asked Khorsh about the rates for portage and transportation. "I hope you can translate for me. I've been practicing my Gozashtandou, but when they all start to chatter at once, it's just a buzz of noise."

"*Com gôsto!* Permit me to recommend litters instead of carriages. During the Festival of Dashmok, traffic is such that you will find litters more practical."

"Oh, yes, the Festival. We timed our arrival for it, and we plan to attend the grand ballet. Yes, Mr. Kosambi?"

The plump Indian had oozed quietly up. "While you are viewing these pagan orgies, Mr. Reith, I trust you will also bring them to the Church of the Lords of Light. You should show them not only the past of this backward planet but also the future, which I am sure will be a brighter one. Compared to the temple of Dashmok nearby, our fane is an humble one, but it represents the true enlightenment."

"Thank you," said Reith. "When will there be a service or meeting or whatever you call it?"

"The day after tomorrow, at high noon. Your presence will be most welcome."

"I'll try to work it into our schedule."

After a wait, a small red-sailed coaster pulled out from the wharf. Captain Ozum slipped the *Zaidun* into the vacated dock, while Krishnans on other waiting craft screamed maledictions. Reith saw what Khorsh had meant by the gods' providing portage and transport. As soon as those on shore realized that the *Zaidun* carried passengers, they swarmed towards that part of the wharf, shouting. Some proclaimed their might and skill as porters or chairmen; some offered services as guides; others waved articles of merchandise.

Reith lined up his tourists, saying: "Stick together and carry your own small hand luggage. We're taking litters."

"Huh?" said Pride. "What's that?"

"Sedan chairs."

The gangplank was thrust over the side. Two of the *Zaidun*'s boatmen stood at the shore end with belaying pins, to discourage unauthorized boarders.

With his heart nervously pounding, Reith stepped up on the gangplank and called in Gozashtandou: "I want twelve porters!"

From the shoving, shouting mob, Reith chose his dozen. He passed them, one at a time, aboard the ship.

Then he lined them up on deck and explained that they were going to Haftid's Inn in the Shodsir. When they seemed to understand, he went ashore to round up chairmen. The tourists straggled up the plank after him. He was hiring his litters when Shirley Waterford spoke:

"Fearless, I can't ride in one of those things."

He turned. "Why not?"

"It's not decent, using people as beasts of burden. It's a kind of racism."

"Oh, my God, Shirley, don't start that now! This is the local custom, and we're expected to follow it. Besides, if we don't hire these poor fellows, how will they make their living?"

"I don't care; I just won't do it. It's an insult to human dignity. Why can't I take this carriage?"

The harried Reith asked the hackney driver for his price. The reply was in such strong Majburo dialect that Reith had to find Khorsh to translate.

When Miss Waterford was in the carriage, Considine and Turner decided that they, too, would prefer to ride behind an aya than be jounced in a litter. They scurried to the carriage and leaped in. Their chairman broke into voluble protests.

"What are they saying, Father Khorsh?" asked Reith.

"They say you have a legitimate contract with them, my son. They say you owe them for the portage, whether or not they carry these two earthmen."

Reith restrained himself from pulling his coppery hair. "What should I do? Pay them for the trip or tell them to go to Hishkak?"

"Permit me to ponder, my son. Ah! I think I have it. In your haste, you neglected to order transport either for yourself or for me."

"I was going to walk, to watch the porters. I'm sorry to have forgotten about you."

"In that case, let us occupy the two vacant chairs, thereby satisfying everyone, as Kurdé the Wise is said to have done in the legend."

"If none of my people or their baggage gets lost."

The litter resembled a telephone booth with a seat inside and a pair of wooden shafts extending fore and aft. Reith squirmed into the seat, getting tangled in his sword. The two chairmen, each of whom wore a leather harness depending from his shoulders to take some of the weight, stooped and hoisted the chair.

The procession set out. Reith craned his neck out the window to see how his convoy was doing. He was in the middle of the string of litters. After the litters came the porters, and after the porters, the carriage.

The column plunged into the streets beyond the waterfront. These streets were so narrow and crooked that the chairman had to crowd to one side to let pedestrians squeeze past. Because none of these streets ran straight for more than two blocks, Reith soon lost sight of the ends of his column.

When the route straightened out enough to allow a clear view to the rear, the carriage was not to be seen. The porters were plodding along with their loads; but the coach, with Shirley Waterford and the dear boys, was gone.

Reith wondered whether the vehicle was stuck at a corner, or had been caught in a riot, or had been attacked by kidnappers. He asked himself whether he ought to run back. Then he committed his missing tourists to the mercy of Dashmok. If they got lost, it would be their own stupid fault.

Roqir was setting in the full scarlet-and-purple glory of a Krishnan sunset when the litters drew up at a nondescript stone-and-timber building, with the skull of some Krishnan beast above the door. A hand-lettered wooden sign bore a row of fishhook characters, looking something like Arabic and something like shorthand. Reith guessed that they gave the name of Haftid's Inn.

Reith spent a frantic half-hour paying off the porters and the chairmen and collecting his tourists and their baggage. There was no sign of the carriage. At last, while Reith was wondering how to organize a search party, the sextuple clop of an aya's hooves resounded, and the carriage arrived. The press of traffic had thinned with the arrival of supper hour.

"Got caught in a jam," said Considine. "I thought we left earth to get away from these, but.... Hey, where's my little blue case?"

Considine was examining the pile of baggage. Reith knew the case in question. In it, Maurice Considine kept the ornaments and jewelry with which he enhanced his looks. Reith, too, failed to find the case.

"God damn it!" yelled Considine. "One of these gooks stole it! I'll sue—I'll—"

"Calm down, Maurice," said Reith. "I told you to carry small hand luggage. If you didn't—"

"Oh, screw you! Some of that junk was valuable! I'll raise hell! I won't stand for it!"

"Looks as if you'd have to," said Reith. "Now I've got to see to our accommodations. Stay here, everybody. Father Khorsh, will you come along?"

Reith pushed through swinging doors and entered the common room of Haftid's Inn. One side was for eating and drinking, with benches and long tables. A few customers sat at these. The other side included some crude stools and a large desk. Behind the desk sat a stout Krishnan running calculations with an abacus and writing them down with pen and ink. Reith gave his name and said in careful Gozashtandou:

"We have a reservation for sixteen, thirteen *Ertsuma* and three Krishnans, in the name of the Magic Carpet Travel Agency." He flourished a paper.

34

The Krishnan glowered up. "No room."

"What?" Reith turned to Khorsh, who corroborated the statement. "But—but I have a definite reservation, with a deposit paid in advance!" Reith waved the paper under the Krishnan's nose.

The Krishnan, whom Reith supposed to be Haftid himself, flapped his hands in the Krishnan equivalent of a shrug. "All full. Festival of Dashmok."

"But I have your own signature here! Get the other people out!"

"I cannot. Too bad." The Krishnan returned to his accounts.

"Now look here, Master Haftid—" said Reith in rising anger. He touched the Krishnan's shoulder.

"Do not, my son!" said Khorsh.

Haftid looked up with a sudden glare. He rose slowly, towering over Reith. "Get ye gone, *Ertsu*! We are full, and that's that!" He pointed doorward.

Enraged, Reith was tempted to draw the sword that clanked about his legs. The fit quickly passed as he recalled that, in a strange city, lost among thousands of beings of another species, he and his tourists could easily drop out of sight for good and all. He cursed himself for not having foreseen this contingency.

In desperation, he turned to Khorsh. "You heard, Father?" he said in Portuguese. "What does one do in a case like that? On earth I'd have some idea, but not here."

Khorsh spread his hands. "I can say very little, my son. He can claim that some guests unexpectedly prolonged their stay, and the law does not let him evict them for a later arrival. You could sue him in the civil courts for the return of the deposit, but that would take years and cost many times the amount at issue."

Reith turned back to the innkeeper and spoke slowly, in the most polite voice he could manage: "Master Haftid, will you do me the goodness to recommend another inn, where I can lodge my people?"

Haftid looked up from his accounts. "I could recite some names, my good foreigner, but 'twould avail you little. All, including those accepting earthmen as guests, are replete with multitudes arriving for the Festival. In every hostelry, be it manor house or hovel, ye'll find folk sleeping on pallets in the common room, for want of better lodging."

Considine called from the doorway: "Hey, Fearless, how much longer you going to keep us standing out here?"

Reith turned back to Khorsh. "Father, have you any idea of where I could put my people? I could doss down on the floor, but I can't ask it of them."

The priest spread hands in resignation. "Alas, my son, I know little of the local hospices. When I travel, I can always put up at a temple; but such accommodations are not open to laymen."

Reith racked his brains. Then he remembered the words of Pierce Angioletti at Novorecife: "If you get into trouble in Majbur, go to see Gorbovast. . . . he can fix anything."

"Master Haftid," said Reith, "will you be so kind as to direct me to the office of Commissioner Gorbovast?"

Now that he no longer faced a confrontation, the innkeeper became more agreeable. "Out the front door, turn left, go to the first crossing, turn right, straight ahead two blocks, and there it is. 'Twere unlikely ye'll find Gorbovast so late in the day, for already Roqir's disk does osculate the far horizon."

Reith made Haftid repeat the directions. Then he hurried out. His tourists set up an outcry, all asking questions: What was wrong? Was there a hitch? Where was he going to put them? Why hadn't the agency made better arrangements? Where was his efficiency? When did they eat? Considine yelled: "Where's my little blue case?"

"You'll have to sit on your luggage for a while, folks," he said. "I'll be back as soon as I can."

He set off at a jog trot, holding his scabbard in his left hand to keep it from tripping him. Dodging beggars and pimps, he soon reached the area to which he had been directed. Then, unable to read the signs over the doors, he realized that he could not tell one office from another. He had a horrid vision of trying every door in the block and asking those within, in broken Gozashtandou, for directions.

As he stood in perplexity, working up his nerve, a trio of Krishnans came out of a building a few doors away. With a large key, one of the three locked the door behind him. Two of the three wheeled out vehicles like an adult version of a terran child's scooter.

Reith hurried up to the group, panting. When he could speak, he said: "Beg excuse, sirs, but could you tell me which are office of Commissioner Gorbovast?"

The smallest of the three turned. In the fading light, this proved an elderly Krishnan with tiny wrinkles all over his face and hair faded to pale jade, now turning silvery in the fading light. Instead of answering the question, this one asked:

"*Se fala português? Parlez-vous français?* Do you speak English? *Tum Hindi boltâ ho?*"

"English, if you please," said Reith. "Are you Commissioner Gorbovast bad-Sár?"

"I am he, sir. You are Mr. Reese, of whom I am hearing, wiz a party of travelers from your planet. What can I do for you?"

Reith explained his predicament. Gorbovast said: "Oh, zat is easy. You and your travelers shall stay at my humble house."

"Oh?" said Reith warily. "There are twelve besides myself, and a Duro priest with two attendants."

"Zat is nossing. I have room. Where are zese children of misfortune?"

"At Haftid's. The bastitch wouldn't let us in, even though the agency had sent him a deposit."

Gorbovast smiled and gave the Krishnan equivalent of a shrug. "Zat happen. I sink he is one of zose wiz a prejudice against earsmen, so he was glad of an excuse. Have you dismiss your transport?"

"Yes."

"Well, zen. . . ." Gorbovast spoke in rapid Gozash-tandou to the other two Krishnans, who departed on their scooters.

"Wait, Mr. Gorbovast," said Reith. "How much is all this going to cost us? I have a budget to meet. . . ."

Gorbovast looked pained. "My dear sir, it shall cost you nossing! You are my guests. After all, I am who I am. Now let us go to Haftid's to reassure your people, who must be anxious."

Feeling relieved, Reith walked back to Haftid's with Gorbovast. Roqir had set; but Karrim, the largest of the three moons, was high in the sky, so there was still plenty of light. As Reith approached, the tourists began to yammer. He silenced them with a gesture and introduced Gorbovast.

"I still want my little blue case!" grumbled Maurice Considine.

Privately, Reith was not sure that Gorbovast's hospitality would cost them nothing. His own experience with tours had made him cynical. At the moment, however, there seemed nothing else to do.

The two Krishnans whom Gorbovast had sent away appeared, each with several hackney coaches in tow. Gorbovast's assistants and the drivers loaded the baggage aboard, and the string of carriages set out at a brisk trot through the crooked streets.

In the gathering dusk, the carriages wound through

the city and out a massive fortified gate. In the suburb, they turned into a graveled driveway and drew up outside a big square structure with blank outside stone walls.

"My humble home," said Gorbovast, waving the tourists in through a small, thick door.

The house was built in the form of a hollow square, so it looked able to stand a minor siege. When he passed through the short tunnel beyond the door, Reith found himself in a spacious courtyard, where flowers bloomed and fountains tinkled. There were other Krishnans, whom Gorbovast introduced. First was his wife; then sons, daughters, and in-laws. The children of these raced about, yelling, in some Krishnan children's game.

"Wow!" said John Turner. "He can call it a hovel, but it looks more like a palace to me. We sure were lucky."

Professor Mulroy's dry old academic voice spoke out: "Charles Darwin, writing of his *Beagle* voyage, said that a traveler should learn to be suspicious; but that he would also discover how many kind-hearted people there are, who would extend him disinterested assistance. This appears to be a case in point."

Gorbovast's servitors took the baggage and led the earthlings to their rooms, as if the sudden descent of sixteen unexpected guests were the most natural thing in Krishna.

"My friends," said Gorbovast after supper, "let us consider ze plans for your stay. What do you propose to do tomorrow, Mr. Reese?"

"I thought I'd take them on a general sightseeing tour of the city," said Reith.

"If I may make a suggestion, you might do better to put zat off for one day."

"Why?"

"Because ze city will be at its most crowded tomorrow, which is a general holiday. Ze shops will be mostly closed, and you will not be able to see much because of ze press of people. Ze day after would be better."

"Then what do you think we should do tomorrow?"

"I have ze idea. I suppose you allow your people a day for shopping?"

"Oh, yes. We had figured on doing that the day before the *Sárbez* sails, three days from now."

"Ze shopping in Majbur during ze festival is bad at best, especially if you do not speak ze language. Ze crowds, ze noise! Sometime a fight begins among ze religious ensusiasts, and zen it is not good for earsmen to be zere. We have some ignorants, full of barbarous racial prejudices."

"Then, how—"

"I can get word to ze merchants, to bring zeir goods here to zis house. You tell me what sort of sings you want to buy, and you shall make your choices in peace and safety."

When most of the tourists approved this plan, Reith assented. Next morning witnessed a procession of merchants from Majbur, spreading their wares in Gorbovast's courtyard. When he saw that the shopping was under control, with Gorbovast as interpreter, Reith went back to Majbur with Khorsh and Khorsh's servants, in Gorbovast's private coach. Saying he had business in one of the temples, the priest left Reith but promised to rejoin the group the following day. Reith hunted up the berth of the *Sárbez* to confirm his reservations and the sailing date.

Reith returned to Gorbovast's mansion in the afternoon, as a couple of the merchants were loading their carts to return to the city. Nearby stood Maurice Considine, examining a new sword and trying to communicate by sign language with a merchant.

"Fearless!" said Considine. "Maybe you can make this gook understand. I'll buy his sword, since I've got to have one; but I still think he's a robber. He wants three times as much as that Krishnan at Novorecife."

In halting Gozashtandou, Reith passed the message on to the merchant, who spread his hands.

"What expects this *Ertsu*?" said the swordseller. "All prices are up because of the Festival. Moreover, with the vast commission of twenty-five per centum, which Master Gorbovast charges us poor merchants, I needs must elevate my prices thus to show any profit whatsoever. Thinks this wight from far and barbarous worlds that I'll arm him with a blade of fine Mikardando steel for nought? True, Dashmok enjoins upon his followers the virtue of charity; but as says Nehavend, charity begins at home—"

Reith held up a hand to check the flow of oratory in rolling, rhythmic, guttural Gozashtandou. "He said prices are up because of the festival and because Gorbovast nicks him one quarter of it as commission. Sounds like our native earth; our charming host isn't going to be out of pocket on our account."

"What?" yelled Considine. "Why, the lousy crook! Bringing us out here, saying it's all free, and turning these vultures loose on his captive market! They're all crooks!"

"What are you crabbing about? They do it back home."

The remark only further infuriated Considine. "And here it's a whole day since one of 'em stole my little blue case, and you haven't done a thing about it. What sort of police have they got? I'll find somebody to translate and go to 'em myself to make a stink. I'll tell 'em we earthmen could wipe this crummy city off the map with one bomb! I'll get some action out of this bunch of lying thieves if you can't. I'll. . . ."

41

A weather-beaten Krishnan of vaguely familiar aspect approached on foot from the highway. Racking his brain, Reith recognized Captain Ozum of the *Zaidun*. The riverboat skipper accosted Considine, saying in bad Portuguese:

"Senhor, is this not yours?"

From under his arm, he produced the missing blue case, explaining: "I found it in your cabin this morning. I looked for you all over Majbur, until someone told me ye were here."

"Oh," said Considine, when Reith had translated. After a moment's hesitation, Considine muttered "*Obrigado*" and turned back to the swordseller to pay for his new blade.

"He is speechless with gratitude," said Reith to the captain. "Anyway, let me thank you most sincerely. Would you accept a small gift?"

He pressed a silver kard on Ozum, who made a show of declining but finally accepted the coin. The captain bade Reith a ceremonious farewell, cast a scornful glance at Considine, and swung into a departing cart.

"This," said Reith, "is the temple of Dashmok, the god of dancing and fun and the tutelary deity of Majbur. Before we go in, you will have to take off your shoes."

"You mean," said Maurice Considine, "leave 'em outside, where anybody could steal them?"

"Yes. The doorkeepers, those tall fellows with the spears, will watch them."

"I still don't trust any of these gooks," growled Considine. "I'll take mine with me." He removed his shoes but hung them around his neck by tying the laces together.

"Boy," said Valerie Mulroy, regarding the stalwart, olive-skinned doorkeepers, "they look as if they could do a woman a world of good."

"Keep your mind on higher things," said Reith. "This is a religious center, so lower your voices. Don't touch anything. Father Khorsh, what did you say was the customary donation?"

After a wait in the vestibule, Reith's gaggle was taken in tow by a young Krishnan acolyte. The visitors exclaimed over the gilded magnificence of the interior, the intricate floral tracery on the walls, the colorful murals, and the columns inlaid with patterns of mother-of-pearl and glittering semiprecious stones of scarlet and green and azure.

The acolyte knew his lecture but tended to rattle it off without pauses for translation. Moreover, he spoke too fast and in too strong a Majburo accent for Reith to follow. Khorsh had to translate into Portuguese to Reith, who rendered that version into English for his people. When Reith asked the acolyte to repeat something he had missed, the Krishnan got confused, went back to the beginning of his speech, and started over.

At the far end of the cella stood the main statue of the jolly god, cross-legged, pot-bellied, grinning, and thrice life size. In front of this statue rose a pedestal of onyx. On this shaft, lit by lamplight focused by concave mirrors, gleamed a replica of the big statue, a mere ten centimeters high and made of a green translucent substance.

"This," said the acolyte, indicating the statuette, "is our most sacred property, carved from a single *balzhik* stone by the artistic demigod Khorbizé, in the days of the Kalwm Empire. It is on this image that we focus our current of etheric force when we pray to Dashmok."

"What does he mean by a *balzhik*?" asked Reith.

The priest spoke to the acolyte, who volubly replied. Then Khorsh said: "It is just the *balzhik*. I do not know

43

what you would call it."

"Nothing but a hunk of green glass," said Silvester Pride.

Aimé Jussac screwed a jeweler's loupe into his eye socket. "Ask him, please, if I may take a close look."

"He says okay, if you don't touch," said Reith.

Jussac stepped close and peered, then turned and put away the loupe. "Either it is an emerald of surpassing size and brilliancy, or the Krishnan art of synthetic gems is in advance of ours."

"Gee!" said Pride. "Can I look, too?"

"Don't drool on it, Silvester," murmured Considine.

"Listen, jerk—" began Pride loudly, but Mrs. Whitney Scott shushed him.

"Come on," said Reith. "We're due at Kosambi's chapel in a quarter-hour Krishnan."

The chapel of the Lords of Light was a large, bare room, which the sect had rented a block from the temple of Dashmok. There had been some effort, with hangings and religious pictures, to give the place a sacerdotal air, but the effect was still depressing.

There were no chairs. Thirty-odd Krishnans sat on the floor in rows, facing the far end of the room. There behind a lectern stood Ganesh Kosambi, in an orange-yellow robe.

"Welcome, kind friends!" said Kosambi, beaming, as Reith and the tourists straggled in. "Sit wherever you like."

The travelers folded themselves up on the floor. Kosambi renewed his discourse in Gozashtando, pausing betimes to give a summary in English. The talk appeared to be a sermon of the sort that one could hear almost any week in a terran house of worship, exhorting the congregation to refrain from lying, theft, assault, and murder, to be good to their kin, kind to their neighbors, and hospitable to strangers, and to practice all the other conventional virtues. It was high-minded but stupefyingly dull.

Silvester Pride muttered: "Bullshit."

Kosambi ended his discourse. The congregation sang in Gozashtandou.

"Now," said Kosambi, "My new friends, this is a part of our ritual I wish you would join in. When you hear me call out: *shar pu'án!*, please to cover your eyes and bow your faces to the floor. The reason is that we shall pray for one of the Lords of Light to manifest himself in this room, and some time one of them might do so. Then, if your eyes were not covered, you might be blinded by his glory."

Kosambi switched back to Gozashtandou. When he ended a passage with a loud "*Shar pu'án!*" Reith bowed his head and covered his eyes.

Kosambi's prayer continued for half a minute. Then the Indian said: "All right, my friends, you may look up now."

Reith stared around. With grunts of discomfort, his tourists were changing their positions from kneeling to sitting. At first he saw nothing wrong. Then a feeling grew upon him that something was missing. He counted his people and realized that Silvester Pride had vanished.

Behind the lectern, Kosambi had launched into another sermon. Reith became impatient. Loath as he was to interrupt, he wished to show his tourists several more local sights before returning to Gorbovast's house. Further, he did not trust Pride on his own.

A rising clamor came from the street outside. Feet pounded on the stair. Pride burst into the room in stocking feet, holding the emerald figurine of Dash-mok. After him came the two guards from the temple, spears at ready, and after them several white-robed priests. The screaming rose until Reith could understand nothing.

"Save me!" mouthed Pride, ducking behind Reith to avoid a thrust from one of the spears.

Reith hesitated, wondering whether to draw his sword. He dismissed that idea at once. As the guard drew back his spear for another jab, Reith placed himself in front of the Krishnan, spreading his arms and shouting one of the few Gozashtando words he could recall: "*Astoi!* Halt!"

The guards paused. Kosambi and his assistant were wrangling furiously with the priests of Dashmok. Reith's tourists added their voices to the din.

"*'Irim!* Quiet!" yelled Reith. When the noise had subsided a little, he added: "Father Khorsh, you must interpret. Ask one of Dashmok's folk what happened."

Khorsh talked to the oldest priest and said: "My son, their tale is that your Senhor Pride came back to the temple after the rest of you had departed. He reverently took off his shoes and entered. Knowing him by sight from the previous visit, the guards thought no harm in it. The next thing they knew, the alarm sounded to indicate the theft of the image. Then out the door comes the Senhor Pride, flying with the idol in his hand. Naturally, they pursued the blasphemer."

"What have you to say, Silvester?" asked Reith.

"I never meant to steal the damned thing! I just wanted a good look at it. On earth it would be worth half a million. Besides, I got bored with the sermon. So I went back in and picked it off the post to see it better. Well, there's some sort of clockwork alarm in the pillar, with a little knob sticking up through a hole in the top. The statue sits on this knob, and when you pick it up all hell breaks loose. This thing went off like an alarm clock, and all these priests came boiling out of their holes. I don't understand their lingo, but it sounded like they wanted to boil me in oil. So I ran for it. I didn't dare take time to try to put the statue back, and I didn't want to drop it for fear of busting it. Here, let 'em take it!"

Pride thrust out the figurine. The oldest priest snatched the statue. Then another priest clattered up the stairs, followed by four Krishnans in the red-and-blue uniforms of the day watch. These laid hands on Pride.

"They say he is under arrest," said Khorsh. "They are taking him to headquarters."

Pride was marched out, complaining: "Hey, don't you guys even let a man go get his shoes?"

Besides the policemen, the prisoner, the temple guards, the priests, and Reith's tourists, Ganesh Kosambi and his congregation came along, too. Other curious Majburuma joined the procession, until over a hundred arrived at police headquarters.

Hours were spent in confusing procedures. The magistrate denied Pride bail, on the ground that as a foreigner he had no local kith or kin to be responsible for him.

The Reith clapped a hand to his forehead in anguish at his own stupidity. "Father Khorsh!" he said. "Can you find me someone to take a message to Gorbovast?"

Khorsh summoned an urchin, who departed on a run with a sheet from Reith's pocket notebook in his grimy fist. Soon Gorbovast appeared.

"*Quel poisse! Ai Râm!* Holy stars!" cried Gorbovast. "What have your people been getting zemselves into now, Mr. Reese?"

When things had been explained, Gorbovast engaged the magistrate in a long, low-voiced conversation. At last he turned back.

"He has decided zat, in view of ze peculiar circumstances, he will let Mr. Pride go wiz a fine of one sousand karda, half of which will be paid to ze temple for damages."

"It'll wipe me out!" said Pride. "I won't be able to buy so much as a postage stamp for the rest of the trip."

"If Mr. Pride prefers," said Gorbovast, "ze police will turn him over to ze priests. Zey have very ingenious messods of punishing blashphemers."

As Pride counted out most of the gold in his purse, one of the younger priests burst into impassioned speech.

"He say," reported Gorbovast, "zat Pride should be given to zem for proper penances. He say if ze magistrate will not do it, ze priests will seize him when he leave ze headquarters. Now ze magistrate ask your plans. . . . He say, if you will take Mr. Pride direct to ship, put him on board, and stay zere wiz ze rest of your people until it sail, ze police will protect you to ze pier. After zat, if you go ashore, you are on your own," Gorbovast gave a dry chuckle. "Zere is a big dispute in Majbur just now over separation of church and state. Your man is lucky; ozzerwise he would not get off so easy. I will send ze baggage to ze ship."

Another procession formed, from police headquarters to the *Sárbez*'s pier. In front marched Silvester Pride, surrounded by a cordon of eight watchmen. Outside this cordon surged a dozen priests of Dashmok, glaring at Pride and watching for a break in the cordon so that they could snatch him from his escort. After this group came the rest of the crowd, including Reith and his tourists.

At the pier, Reith and his people bid Gorbovast a hasty farewell and went aboard. After the rest of the crowd had dispersed, two watchmen remained to guard the gangplank.

Captain Denaikh was not pleased. " 'Twill cost you eke," he grumbled, "since I must feed this troop for an extra day. Besides and moreover, I'd fain have no lubbers prancing about my deck whilst we're loading, lest he set himself beneath some descending tun and be smashed, like as a bug beneath a boot heel. Understand ye, good my sir?"

As Reith herded his people into their cabins in the deckhouse, Pride said: "Hey, Fearless, you mean we've got to stay cooped up all day tomorrow? We can't see the ballet, with the little priestesses waggling their pretty bare tits?"

"No; we'll miss the show."

"That's not fair! I paid for that along with the rest of the trip."

Reith grabbed Pride's lapels. "Look, you blithering ass! You got us into this. By God, if I could figure how, I'd ship you back to Novorecife and tell you to sue the agency if you didn't like it. If you want to go ashore and take your chances with those guys—" (Reith pointed at the line of white-clad priests, waiting hopefully on the pier) "—go right ahead, and I hope they tear you limb from limb!"

"Why, you—you jerk!" cried Pride. "Take your hands off me, damn it! You dare talk to me like that— I'll have your job when we get home! I'll turn in a report on you that'll—"

Valerie Mulroy came to Reith's defense. "Mr. Pride, after you caused all this trouble, and Fearless saved us from being massacred, you want to blame him? Fergus is a nice boy, and you're a silly old fart!"

"She is right," Santiago Guzmán-Vidal chimed in. "Shut up and go away, you *sapillo*!"

Several other tourists spoke up in Reith's behalf. Pride subsided and entered his cabin.

IV.

RIOT IN ZAMBA

Across the turquoise waters of the sparkling Sadabao Sea, beneath a yellow sun in a bluish-green sky, the *Sárbez* plodded her stately way. Since the weather was fair, Reith's tourists were all, for once, in good humor. None had ever voyaged by square-rigger before, since no such craft still sailed the terran seas. They therefore found the details of the ship's operation fascinating.

They shuddered at the sight of Krishnan sailors' laying aloft to furl or break out sail while swaying on footropes ten or fifteen meters above the deck. They talked of pirates and hornpipes and tacks. They mangled the nautical terminology of their respective languages.

The morn of their first night brought the *Sárbez* in sight of the island of Zamba. By mid-morning, they stood outside the harbor of Reshr, the capital, where onion-domed towers loomed over a gleaming marble

wall. Captain Denaikh hove to and furled sail, while a
boat came alongside with a pilot and a harbor
inspector. The latter's badge of office was an
ornamental key of silver and colored glass around his
neck.

Reith showed the inspector the papers for his party.
With Khorsh interpreting, the official said:

"In the name of King Penjird the Second, I welcome
you to the kingdom of Zamba. His Majesty graciously
condescends to grant you and your party an audience
tomorrow afternoon, at three hours past midday."

"We thank His Majesty very much," said Reith in
stumbling Gozashtandou. "We shall be there. If there
be no complications, we are fain to come ashore today
to view your beautiful city."

"You are welcome to do so," said the inspector.
"You may wish to view the *shánenesb* this afternoon."

Reith asked Khorsh: "What was that last word
again?"

As the priest explained it, a *shánenesb* was
something like a terran horse show, in which Krishnan
domestic animals of several species were put through
their paces.

The inspector shouted to the captain, who shouted
to a petty officer, who shouted to a seaman, who ran up
a flag. A pair of harbor craft, which had been waiting in
the offing, approached. They were oar-powered tugs—
heavy rowboats, like small galleys, with a pair of
brawny Krishnans pulling each oar. With much
yelling, slap of bare feet on decks, and rattle of pulley
blocks, lines were belayed to each of the tugs. These
craft then towed the *Sárbez* into the inner harbor.

As the ship, moving with glacial slowness, neared
the pier, John Turner plucked Reith's sleeve. "Hey,
Fearless! What's that thing? Fry my guts if it doesn't
look like a steamboat—an old-time paddle-wheeler!"

Turner handed his binoculars to Reith, who looked and turned to the inspector, saying: "What is that, sir?"

"Oh," said the inspector. "That is the new ship, hight *Mokinam*, of Prince Ferrian of Sotaspé. This potentate does even now pay a visit of state to our majestic sovran. Know you the tale? This Ferrian, a wight of pith and spirit, has purloined from you *Ertsuma* a mort of secrets of the engineering crafts. By means of these, this saucy swain does raise his minikin isle to be the mightiest power maritime of the Middle Sea. They say he's even built a kind of flying machine, propelled through the air by combustion of *yasuvar* pollen, wherewith we build fireworks to celebrate holidays.

"Time was when he and our gracious ruler were in hot and hostile rivalry; but, happily, that's now composed. The lordly twain do seek to cement their love by mutual alliance. And—oh—ere I forget— Prince Ferrian were vastly wroth, did one of you honored visitors employ a picture-taking machine upon his proud ship *Mokinam*. He fears a repetition of his disaster of a few years back."

"What disaster?" asked Reith.

"Why, with the help of a renegade *Ertsu*, he'd built a similar craft, clept *Kerukchi*. Getting wind of this, the *Ertsuma* of Novorecife swooped upon Majbur, hired a ship, and caught and burned the *Kerukchi* in open sea." The Krishnan made the curious noise that served as a chuckle. "By this outrageous violation of the Krishnan nations' sovran rights, they thought to stop the spread of their knowledge scientifical, fearing lest we Krishnans overtake them in this race for wisdom and rape them of their advantage in dealing with us. But little they recked of our yaresome princeling! Having a set of plans for the *Kerukchi* safe at home in Sotaspé, he escaped the wreck and set himself to

53

fabricate another craft, of design improved in light of
his experience with the first. Yonder lies the terror of
the sapphire Sadabao!"

Reith turned to his tourists. "He says, no photo-
graphs of the steamship." He looked hard at Otto
Schwerin. *"Kein Bild!"*

Schwerin smiled vaguely and bobbed his head.

Ashore, it took Reith over an hour to round up
transport for his tourists and another to locate the
shánenesb. On the outskirts of Reshr was an open area
with an elliptical racecourse and a small grandstand.
There were concessions and dust and noise. A
conjuror, a juggler, a seller of nostrums, and a puppet
show were all going full blast in noisy competition.

Reith would have liked to buy tickets for seats in the
grandstand, but the stand was already full of upper-
class Krishnans. The sword-clanking males were in
cloaks of emerald and purple and scarlet over the
Krishnan loin garment. This could be either an
oversized diaper, or a kind of divided kilt. The females
wore bare-breasted dresses, inciting Pride to utter bad
jokes. The terrans had to wriggle through a much
larger crowd of smellier and more drably-clad
Krishnans, who lined the fence on either side of the
grandstand.

The Krishnans stared at their exotic visitors but
then turned their attention back to the field within the
race track, puffing cigars of ultra-strong Krishnan
tobacco. Reith thought that, if early terran visitors had
introduced tobacco before the I. C. had clamped down
the technological blockade, they should at least have
let in soap as well. The perfumes used by even poor
Krishnans failed to cover the aroma of unsoaped
Krishnan. Khorsh said:

"Senhor Reith, they tell me the races are already

over. The next event will be a drill by the Royal Zamban Lancers."

Reith and his people stood, shifting from foot to foot, while on the field Krishnan boys ran about with scoops and buckets collecting animal droppings. At last, from the stables in the distance, the lancers, in uniforms of black and gold with silvered cuirasses, on matched black ayas, trotted into the field. A brass band played.

The soldiers maneuvered their ayas in elaborate square, circular, and pinwheel formations, crossing in and out like square dancers. They ended with a charge down the field, in double rank with lances leveled. At the end, they brought their mounts to a simultaneous skidding stop.

After the drill came a series of class judgings. A group of riders of yearling shomals trotted out, put their mounts through paces, and lined up before the judges, who sat on a row of folding chairs in front of the grandstand. Then came a class of six-gaited ayas. . . .

Reith's people began to stir and grumble. After the first impact of the pageantry had worn off, there were murmurs against the leisureliness of the program, especially since they had to wait for Khorsh to translate each item of news and for Reith to translate Khorsh.

"Should have brought my shooting stick," said Mrs. Whitney Scott. "I'm too old to stand all afternoon."

"Snails are fast compared to this," growled Maurice Considine. "Too much dead time between each event and the next. Have a swig, Fearless?" He extended a flask of kvad, which he had bought from a refreshment stand behind the grandstand.

"No, thanks," said Reith. "I need my wits. Well, if we're all agreed to go—"

"Hey!" said Considine. "What are they doing now?"

"A jumping contest," explained Khorsh. The priest pointed to the field, where workmen were setting up hurdles and other props. Others were filling a wide, shallow trench with water from a tank wagon. "This will be for aya hunters. The riders must follow a course like this—" (he made looping motions in the air) "—and stay within the markers—those barrels."

"Gotta see this," said Considine, weaving slightly. "Used to do that kind of thing myself. Right, John?"

"Oh, sure," said Turner.

Reith wondered how much kvad Considine had drunk. Certain Krishnan plants had the property, when properly treated, of fermenting to a liquor much stronger than any terran wine, albeit lower in alcoholic content than distilled terran liquors. Although the principle of distillation was known, Krishnans did not distill their booze. They had no need to.

The first contestant trotted out on his horned, six-legged mount, colored like a palomino horse. Some of Reith's tourists snickered at the sight of the rider's headgear, which bore a startling resemblance to a terran derby hat with a chin strap.

"It is a kind of padded leather helmet," explained Khorsh, "in case the rider should fall off on his head."

The contestant broke into a canter, cleared a hurdle, brought his mount around in a tight circle, cleared another hurdle, ducked beneath a cross-bar set up in his path, cleared the water hazard in a long jump, galloped between a pair of posts just wide enough to allow passage, and so on through the intricacies of the course. When he finished, the crowd whistled to show appreciation. In their chairs, the judges scribbled notes.

After six more contestants had put their mounts through the course, Reith asked: "Father Khorsh, how many more of these?"

"Five more, my son. After that come the finals,

when the three best jumpers will compete; and after that the carriage-driving contest."

"I guess we've seen enough of this," said Maurice Considine. "That lash—last guy wasn't much good. I can ride better."

"Okay," said Reith. "We'll watch one more, unless somebody wants to see the carriage-drivers."

"I would like the carriages if I was not so tired from these esstanding," said Pilar Guzmán-Vidal.

"Hey!" cried Considine. "Look at that!"

The latest contestant had put his piebald aya at the second hurdle. The animal refused the jump, spilling its rider into the dust. The aya turned and started back towards the stables, its empty stirrups swinging.

"I'll show 'em!" shouted Considine. The young man climbed over the fence.

Reith yelled: "Hey, Maurice! Come back!"

Considine ran to the trotting aya and swung into the saddle with the adroitness of a cowboy. Cries arose from the crowd. Khorsh told Reith:

"They are saying, is he a clown disguised as an earthman?"

It was one thing to mount the beast and another to control it thereafter. As if aware that it had been forked by no proper Krishnan, the aya spun round and round. Then it set off at a mad gallop, weaving among the hurdles and other obstacles. Considine clung to the saddle.

Turner pulled Reith's sleeve. "Save him, Fearless! He'll be killed!"

"How the hell do you expect me—" began Reith.

A general outcry drowned his voice. The aya, running past the judges, went into buck-jumps with all six legs. At the second jump, Considine flew off and came down on the lap of one of the judges, whose chair collapsed with a crash.

Officials and policemen ran towards the pair, who

sprawled entangled on the wreckage of the chair. Before they reached the place, the judge got up and stood jumping up and down and shaking fists. John Turner's high bleat sounded above the uproar:

"Maurice!"

Turner climbed the fence and ran towards his fallen friend. When he got there, the crowd was thick around Considine. Turner disappeared into the throng.

Reith told his remaining tourists: "Stay where you are!" Then he, too, climbed the fence.

When he pushed his way into the crowd around Considine, Reith found himself in the midst of a furious dispute. The judge who had been sat on was still shouting. A pair of policemen held Considine, now on his feet with dirt on his face. Another pair held Turner. Other Krishnans yelled and shook fists. Some, gesticulating, turned towards Reith, who could not understand a word.

At last, a Krishnan addressed Reith in broken Portuguese: "You boss these *terrestres*?"

"Yes, sir. What—"

"Judge angry. Want take to jail. You come, quick."

"But I have ten others—"

"*Não importa!* You no want head chop, you come."

A gate was opened in the fence, and the crowd pushed through. The police pulled Turner and a limping Considine along.

The argument among the Krishnans, however, had now spread to the spectators. The policemen and their prisoners and the furious judge were blocked by the yammering crowd.

Standing tiptoe, Reith caught a glimpse of Khorsh. "*Ohé*, Father Khorsh!"

The priest pushed through to join him. Reith asked: "What in Hishkak are they hollering about now?"

"Some say, my son, that the earthman should be punished for disrupting the program. Others, on the contrary, say that your man furnished the most amusement of the show and should be rewarded. These are a passionate and disputatious—"

A nearby Krishnan struck another in the face. The victim reeled back and bumped into Khorsh, whom Reith caught and saved from a fall.

"I think, my son," said Khorsh, "you had better gather your folk for a quick retreat."

"But I can't leave—" said Reith.

"Ah, but you can. By the grace of the gods, behold!"

A clash of steel resounded. In the grandstand, a pair of the gentry, caught up in the dispute over Considine, had drawn swords and were having at each other, clang-clang. The policemen holding Considine and Turner released their prisoners to run to the grandstand. While they and others seized and disarmed the fighters, Reith caught Considine and Turner by the arms and hauled them towards the exit gate.

"Stay there!" he commanded, and ran back to round up the rest. As he dodged through the crowd, a wild punch, which one Krishnan had thrown at another, caught him over the ear. He staggered and saw stars but kept on. By the time the forces of order had quelled the disturbance, Reith had his party collected. The priest said:

"You see, my son, the efficacy of prayer. I uttered a humble petition to Bákh, to furnish us a distraction—"

"Oh, God!" said Reith, who had just counted his party. "Where's Otto?"

Mélanie Jussac answered: "The Mr. Schwerin left before Mr. Considine acted the cowpusher. He said he had taken enough pictures here and will meet us at the ship."

Reith pressed knuckles to his head. "If that idiot

doesn't get lost, wandering a strange city where he can't speak the language—well, come on, folks, back to the ship. Keep together, now."

Reith glanced back to see the next hunter trotting out on the field, and then his carriage carried him out of sight of the *shánenesb*. Nobody tried to stop them from leaving. The judge might fume, Reith thought, but the cops were probably glad to see the last of Reith's party before one of these crazy extra-Krishnans touched off another disturbance.

Half a Krishnan hour later, at the pier, Reith's people got down from their carriages and filed aboard the *Sárbez*. Reith was paying off the hackmen when another uproar erupted.

At the base of the pier appeared Otto Schwerin, running. After him came a tall, handsome Krishnan in a silvered breastplate, sword in hand. Behind the pursuer, at a distance, came other armed Krishnans.

Schwerin pounded out on the pier, his cameras swinging on their straps. "*Hilfe!*" he gasped, dodging behind Reith. "Safe me!" He caught the back of Reith's clothing.

"Out of my way!" yelled the armored Krishnan in English.

The swordsman tried to dodge around Reith to get at Schwerin. Schwerin kept circling, clinging to Reith's back, so as to keep Reith between himself and the Krishnan. When a lunge by the Krishnan barely missed Reith's ribs, Reith drew his own sword and knocked the Krishnan's blade aside.

"Oh, you want to fight, too?" snarled the Krishnan.

He aimed a terrific backhanded cut at Reith's neck. Reith parried with a clang. Handicapped as he was by Schwerin's clinging to his back, he beat off, by a hair's breadth, several thrusts and slashes.

The other pursuing Krishnans arrived. Two had

swords, one a halberd, and one a crossbow. Faced by these odds, Reith backed until he found himself on a seaward corner of the pier. Thence he had no place to go but into the oily, débris-littered water.

The Krishnan in the silvery cuirass paused in his attack, breathing hard. The arbalester aimed his crossbow at Reith, shouting in Gozashtandou:

"Drop that sword!"

Reith dropped the sword. Before the armored one could renew his assault, Reith cried: "Aren't you Prince Ferrian?"

"What if I am?"

"Then, will Your Altitude kindly tell me what in hell this is about?"

"This earthman cowering behind you photographed my ship, although you people had been warned not to do so."

"Is that so, Otto?" asked Reith.

"Vell—I—it vass just vun little picture—"

"Look here, Prince, will it satisfy you if he gives you the film? Then no harm will have been done."

Ferrian took his time about answering, while the crossbowman kept his weapon trained on Reith's midriff. At last the prince said:

"I suppose it will, even though I suspect he's a spy of those damned imperialists at Novorecife. But which of those cameras was he using? No, never mind asking. He would lie about it to save his picture of my ship, so he could sell it to Abreu. Take out the films of all of them!"

"*Donnerwetter!* That vill shpoil all the pictures I have took in Reshr—"

"Sorry about that," said Reith. "Let's have 'em, or I'll turn you over to these guys."

Schwerin gave a wail. One by one, his three cameras were opened and the films ripped out. Prince Ferrian sheathed his jewel-hilted sword and held the films up to make sure that all had been thoroughly light-struck. He spoke to his minions, who roughly searched Schwerin. Ferrian explained to Reith: "He might have one of those little cameras no larger than a *ghalok* egg hidden about him."

"Your Highness speaks excellent English for a Krishnan."

Ferrian smiled grimly. "I have visited your planet. You fence well for an earthman."

"Well enough to keep Your Highness from taking my head off. Heggstad at Novorecife beat me black and blue teaching me."

"My apologies, Mr.—ah—"

"Reith, Fergus Reith."

"Well then, Mr. Reith, please excuse my incivility. Legal redress is so slow and uncertain here that, when I suffer a wrong, I am often tempted to right it by self-help. How are they at Novo these days?"

Reith shrugged. "Well enough, as far as I can see."

Ferrian spoke to the other Krishnans, handed them the ruined strips of film, and turned back to Reith. "Your little man seems innocent of more equipment, so I shall let him go. You should keep your people under tighter control."

Reith sighed. "My authority is limited."

Ferrian laughed shortly. "That may do on earth, but not here. Were I a tourist guide, I'd have a stout sergeant-at-arms and an assistant to keep them in order. If any disobeyed, I would have him flogged."

"A lovely idea, sir."

"You earthlings will learn. Again, my apologies." Ferrian gave a stiff little bow. "When some of my projects are further advanced, I shall open Sotaspé to parties like yours. *Adeus!*"

Reith went aboard the *Sárbez* and sought his cabin. He poured a drink of kvad, telling himself that for once he had earned it. He had taken only the first sip when a heavy knock on his door resounded.

"Come forth, O Senhor Reith!" growled Captain Denaikh. "A man from the government demands your presence."

The Krishnan was the inspector who had greeted them on their arrival. After Khorsh had been found to translate, the inspector said:

"I have the honor to bear a message from His supreme Altitude, Penjird the Second, Dour of Zamba. It has come to the notice of our high and mighty potentate that twice in one day has the presence of your churlish barbarians led to public broils and affrays. It is therefore ordained and commanded that all of you shall, on pain of doom most dire, remain upon your ship during the residue of your stay in port. Here is your copy of the order. What is your reply?"

"I don't know. What am I supposed to say?"

"That you humbly beg the pardon of His gracious Altitude for the misconduct of your folk and thank him for his compassionate leniency in not having you all haled ashore to suffer punishment condign."

"Consider it said, sir."

The inspector turned to go. Captain Denaikh spoke angrily to the inspector, who replied in kind. From the occasional Gozashtando word he caught, Reith inferred that the captain was protesting having his passengers aboard all next day, because they would get in the way of his loading. The inspector, adamant, soon departed, leaving Denaikh to stamp and bellow curses. He ripped out a sentence at Reith. Khorsh explained:

"He says, my son, that this is the second time this has happened. If it occur but once more, he will put the lot of you ashore, wherever he be, and sail off without you."

Reith went back to his cabin and took a big drink.

He examined the scroll the official had given him but could make nothing of the fishhooks.

A quarter-hour later, Reith, with more kvad inside him than he usually allowed himself, went around the deck, banging on his tourists' cabin doors. When he had them gathered in the bow of the *Sárbez*, he told them of Prince Ferrian and the governmental order.

Reith expected them to take his side against the two malefactors, Considine and Schwerin, as they had against Silvester Pride. Instead, they capriciously swung round and blamed Reith for the latest imbroglio. They cried:

"You mean we've got to stay aboard all tomorrow?" "We can't see the temples and things?" "The king won't receive us?" "Why didn't you figure this out, Fearless?" "What's the matter with you?" "Damned if I won't go ashore whenever I want to!" "This petty little king can't bully me!" "It's an outrage!" "I'll demand my money back!"

Pride said: "Hey, that means I can't buy another pair of shoes, to take the place of those I lost!"

Only old Mrs. Scott and the Jussacs took Reith's part, and the chorus of complaints drowned them out. Reith guessed that his people were irritable as a result of the long, fatiguing stand at the race track. At last, drunk enough to be reckless, he banged the deck with his scabbard and roared:

"All right, shut up! I've got a thing to say. Twice, you've almost gotten me killed by your damn foolishness.

"Now you'll have to make up your minds, if 'minds' is the word I want. If you wish to quit now and go back to Novorecife, to wait there for the next ship out, that's okay with me."

"How would you get us back?" said Considine. "They won't let us off this tub, and she's bound for Baianch."

"Never mind; I'll make the arrangements. If you prefer to complete the tour, you'll have to agree to obey my orders."

"Thinks he's one of these Krishnan kings," muttered Considine.

Reith mastered an impulse to haul out his sword and give Considine the flat. "And furthermore, if you decide to continue the tour, and if you then cause any more riots, we'll stop right there and start back to Novorecife. Do you all understand?"

After more sullen mutterings, Reith polled his tourists. "Professor Mulroy, do you vote to go on or return?"

All voted to go on despite grumblings about Reith's "dictatorship." Reith snapped:

"If you don't like it, anyone who wants to beat his way back to Novo on his own is welcome to try."

"That's not fair," said Turner. "You can talk to these gooks and we can't."

"That's your problem, laddie. Any takers? No? Okay, we go on. Meeting dismissed.

V.

THE WRONG DOOR

As the *Sárbez* was slowly warped against her pier in Baianch harbor, Reith and his dozen tourists lined the shoreward rail. They were a bedraggled, woebegone-looking lot. Several days of storm at sea had afflicted most of them with excruciating seasickness.

With the nearing of solid ground, however, they began to revive. Some pointed to the cliff that rose above the lower town. Along the brow of this cliff, a massive gray fortification frowned down, with the onion-domed towers of a royal palace projecting above the curtain wall. Behind the fortress, the upper town stretched away towards the base of the promontory on which Baianch was built. Now, save for the tops of temple spires, the upper town was hidden by the loom of the cliff. To right and left of the cape, the darkly forested hills of Dur rolled away.

"It reminds me of Quebec," said Aimé Jussac.

"Look at the soldiers!" said Pilar Guzmán-Vidal.

"Are they going to arrest us, Fearless?"

On the pier, a platoon of uniformed Duruma were drawn up in two ranks, one of crossbowmen and one of pikemen. They wore winged helms, and hauberks of black chain mail over scarlet tunics. Among them stood a group in Duro civilian costume. These folks wore real trousers instead of diapers, and their garments were trimmed with fur. Their complexions were lighter than those of Krishnans of the more southerly nations.

"Don't worry," said Reith. "This looks like a fancy reception. The Regent wants to give us a good time, so more tourists will spend their money here."

As the gangplank slammed into place, a bugle sounded. The soldiers snapped to attention and presented their pikes and crossbows. Led by a very large Krishnan in black, the civilians marched briskly up the gangplank. The leader, who bore a heraldic yeki embroidered in scarlet on the breast of his tunic, strode to the group of tourists and said in Durou:

"Which of you is leader?"

Khorsh translated, pointing to Reith. The huge, black-clad one clicked boot heels, bowed slightly, and shot a hand out to Reith. "Tashian bag-Gárin, at your service."

Trying to remember the differences between Durou and Gozashtandou, Reith replied: "I—ah—Fergus Reith, Your Excellency. We are—ah—honor your greeting by." He noted with surprise that the Regent's black suit, far from reflecting the splendor of his position, was old and threadbare, with visible mends.

"Excellent!" said the Regent. "We have provided you with quarters in the Old Palace, for our inns are not suitable. This even, we would fain offer a formal reception and banquet, if you be not overmuch fatigued by your journey. How say you?"

Reith shot questions at his tourists, then turned

back and bowed. "We shall are delight and honored."

A string of carriages furnished by the Regent bore the party up the slope of narrow, twisting streets, between grim gray battlemented walls, to the Upper City. Beggars, some crippled or mutilated, trotted whining after them.

"Good lord!" said Shirley Waterford. "These people could do with some social justice."

An hour later, they were installed in the crumbly Old Palace, across the street from the New. The towers of the latter they had seen from the ship. The Old Palace was used as an annex to the governmental offices in the New Palace. Their apartments showed signs of having been hastily reconverted from offices into dwellings. Reith could imagine the governmental clerks, grumbling at being ousted, with their files and records, to make room for the foreigners. There had also been some hasty painting and plastering to cover the signs of age.

The New Palace, like the Regent's garb, proved surprisingly shabby. In the reception room, in mid-afternoon, Reith was introduced to the Douri, Vázni bad-Dushta'en. "Douri" could be translated either as "queen" or as "princess," since the customs of most Varasto nations did not permit a female to exercise actual rule.

The nominal head of state of Dur was young, well-shaped, and plump for a Krishnan, with a glittering tiara on her blue-green hair. She wore a gauzy violet gown and had tinted her feathery antennae to match.

Having been instructed in advance, Reith dropped to one knee and kissed the hand she extended. Vázni giggled.

"Rise," she said. "You, fair sir, shall have the first dance with me. How like you my habiliments?"

"Is beautiful—beautiful," said Reith.

69

"Oh, fiddle-faddle! 'Tis last year's—a poor thing but mine own, as says the hero in Saqqiz's *Queen Dejanai*. But flattery, they say, will get you everywhere. Forget not the first dance!"

Reith cast a stricken look at the Regent. He was at best a poor dancer. What with the riding, fencing, and language study that had occupied him at Novorecife, the idea of learning Krishnan dances as well had never occurred to him. In a dazed way, he introduced his tourists, all tricked out in Krishnan finery.

"Master Reese," said Tashian, "if you will have the kindness to stand there, with your people in line behind you, I shall present you and yours. Are we ready? This is our Minister of Mines and Forests, hight Sálegu bam-Morgh...."

The Regent had lined up all his upper bureaucrats— at least two hundred, plus the mates of most—to greet the visitors. The crowd smelled mightily of perfumery.

Reith took a few seconds off from handshaking to ask Khorsh to get a chair for Mrs. Scott. When he turned back, he was startled to see that the next handshaker was another earthman. This was a man of about Reith's age and height, impressively muscled, with light-brown hair and an attractive grin.

Reith missed the name, which the Regent spoke with a strong accent. The terran wrung Reith's hand in a crushing grip, saying:

"I'm Kenneth Strachan, Mr. Reith. I must see you later about the rail trip."

"Are you Scottish?" asked Reith, noting a slight accent.

"Aye. And you're American, despite a good Scots name, eh?"

"My parents came from Scotland, and I belong to the St. Andrews Society at home—"

"Later," said Strachan. "The chief of police of

Baianch is ahint me, eager to shake your hand and get back to chasing malefactors."

Reith met more officials, whose names he had given up trying to remember. Then came a black earthman, tall, lean, and frizz-haired. Unlike the other human beings present, he wore terran clothes.

"I'm Percy Mjipa," he said in a crisp, precise manner. "I'm here to arrange a terran consulate in Baianch. So far, Dur has been spared many visitors from earth; but if they are to have more, there'll be need for a permanent W. F. representative."

Reith said: "Glad to know you, Mr. Mjipa. If I may ask, what part of our planet did you come from?"

"Botswana, in southern Africa. I'm a Mangwato. Try to keep your people up to standard, old boy. Mustn't let the side down in front of non-humans, you know. Many terrans we get here are mere riffraff, who do our image no good."

Mjipa passed on. The end of the line approached. A bar opened for business, and a four-piece orchestra began to thump and tweetle.

"Master Reese," said a voice, "you promised me the first dance." Vázni stood at Reith's elbow.

Reith had not done anything of the sort. Tashian had set him to work greeting bureaucrats before he had had time to answer the princess's initiative. With a mighty effort, he put together a reply in broken Durou:

"I am charmed, Douri. But I not know how Krishnans do dance. You teach, please."

She giggled again. "This were simple, good my sir. Give me your hand. Now you stand *thus* and step *thus*, and then we separate and bow, *thus*. Behold the envoy from Ulvanagh, yonder, with his wife!"

The minuetlike dance turned out less complicated than Reith had feared. Soon he and Vázni were stepping hither and thither, circling, and bowing. Still,

Reith was relieved when the dance ended before he had trodden on somebody's toe and caused an interplanetary incident.

Reith had been so busy struggling on one hand with the dance and on the other with Durou and he was hardly aware of Vázni as a person. Still, when he relinquished her, he felt a pang of jealousy as Maurice Considine stepped up and said in English:

"May I have the next, Your Majesty?"

Vázni laughed at the strange sounds but evidently understood. Soon she and Considine were twirling about on the floor, the latter as if he had done it all his life.

Reith went to the bar, where the Jussacs were going over the refreshments like a pair of vacuum cleaners, and obtained a drink of kvad. Here he got into converse with an elderly Duru who spoke a little Portuguese. The Duru, chief of the Bureau of Resources, explained:

"The Regent is eager to make his kingdom the planet's foremost tourist attraction. We cannot let little powers like Majbur and Sotaspé outdistance us. You as an expert can advise us."

"I shall be glad to give what small help I can," said Reith.

He would have liked to urge flush toilets upon the Krishnans but knew that he could not because of the Saint-Rémy treatment, to which he and his tourists had been subjected. The treatment would tongue-tie them any time they tried to impart technical knowledge to extraterrestrials. He said:

"The main things are to see that the visitors have places to sleep without vermin, and food not too different from what they are used to...."

The dancers left the floor, and servitors carried out chairs and tables. The tables were set in a long U-shaped row. Reith found himself seated at Vázni's left, at the curve of the U, while the Regent sat on her right. The tourists were scattered among the Krishnans, in what Tashian evidently hoped would be a chummy arrangement. Lack of any common speech with their neighbors, however, caused them to eat in rather glum silence. As usual on Krishna, the terrans found some items on the menu inedible. The Duruma politely pretended not to notice.

"Master Reese," said Vázni, "you shall tell me of the strange customs of your native world. I am told that amongst you creatures, the young are born alive, like the young of the aya and the yeki here, instead of being hatched from eggs as with us and other four-limbed living things."

"That quite true, Your Majesty."

"Then how do the young get started in the first place? Does the male go in unto the female to implant his seed, as with us?"

"Well—ah—Your Majesty—ah—yes. That are true."

"Then tell me just how this is done. They say that copulation betwixt an *Ertsu* and a Krishnan is quite possible, even pleasurable. If true, that means their organs must be similar. I am curious; I have never seen an earthman's—why, Master Fergus, are you unwell? Wherefore turns your face so red?"

Despite the strenuous introduction to the pleasures of sex that he had received from Valerie Mulroy, Reith had never fully escaped from the early training of his neo-Puritan parents. He stammered:

"Majesty please excuse me. With—with my bad Durou, might gave wrong information. When I were longer in Dur—"

"Pester not the young earthman, Vázni," growled Tashian. "Too young are you, with such arcane matters to concern yourself."

"Oh, you are ever lecturing me on keeping my

innocence and preserving the purity of our blood line,"
said Vázni. "I am fully grown and should long since
have had a stalwart mate—one who would not make
me wear last year's gown to formal functions."

Tashian leaned forward and spoke to Reith past the
Douri. "Heed her not, Master Reese. She blames me
because I, steadfastly bent on getting her a worthy
husband, have rejected some fribbling suitors, wights
of neither rank nor wit nor heroism. The future prince
consort shall be none but the best!"

"At this rate, I shall perish of eld ere you find him,"
said Vázni. "Nor would this hero ardently press his
suit, once he's seen me in the hideous remnants wherein
you clothe me."

Tashian continued: "Master Reese, Strachan tells
me he must needs return to Zir, the third day hence.
Will your people be prepared to go with him? My
astrologer avers that 'tis a day auspicious."

"As far as I know, we are ready," said Reith. "What
is position of Master Strachan?"

"Assistant engineer on the railroad I'm building to
Zir. Sigvard Lund is chief engineer. Master Strachan is
in Baianch to order more supplies. I trust you can
occupy your people's time for the next two days?"

"I am sure, Excellence. Is enough things here to kept
us busy a long time."

"Good. I shall arrange the *Sárbez*'s sailing for some
days after your return from Zir. Thus will you take in
such local sights as you fail to see this time."

"Your Excellence is very considerate."

As usual in a world without electric light, dinner had
begun well before sunset. Before full dark had fallen,
the guests began to rise, come to the head of the table,
compliment the Regent and the Douri, and be excused.

Kenneth Strachan came up and spoke to the rulers.
Then he said to Reith: "When you've stashed your

trippers, laddie, come back here. You'll find me in the game room."

The game room was small, with a fireplace and five tables for Krishnan board games. At one of these sat Strachan with a goblet of kvad before him. The tables were otherwise unoccupied.

"Sit ye down, Fergus ma lad," he said to Reith. He snapped a finger to the hovering servitor and said in Durou: "A drink for my friend here, and feed the fire a bit." He turned back to Reith. "Old King Dushta'en was a great one for games, but his nephew's too sober by half. All he thinks of is augmenting the might and modernizing the technics of Dur, as well as squeezing every kard until the god on the coin yells for help. You might call him a would-be Krishnan Peter the Great. The rumor is, that's why he dilly-dallies about letting the Douri marry. If she hatches a boy, he's king when he reaches majority, and awa goes Tashy's power to remake his country.

"So, anyway, the game room's nocht but a little private barroom, where few but masell ever come. You're taking your trippers out to the end of the line, at the borders of Zir?"

Strachan had a habit which Reith found disconcerting. Most of the time, he spoke a colorless standard English, much like Reith's own; but every now and then he would slip into broad Scots for a word or a phrase. Reith listed his tourists, told something of their individual peculiarities and requirements, and added:

"It's a long way from Scotland, Mr. Strachan. How did you come to land here?"

Strachan smiled. "His Excellence is daft to modernize his country whether the Duruma want to be modernized or not. One of his projects is this railroad along the shores of the Va'andao to Zir. He hopes to

extend it around the corner to Gozashtand, to join the
main line from Hershid to Qadr and from Majbur to
Jazmurian, if he can ever agree with that fussy little
King Eqrar. And if the stagecoach magnates don't
derail the whole project first, or the old nobility don't
hatch a revolt to pay Tashian back for screeding their
feudal privileges.

"Weel, Tashian sent out word he had good jobs for
Krishnans who could build a railroad. A couple of
rascally Majburuma took him in with extravagant
promises, but their work turned out all wrong. The
roadbed was so rough, not even a push-cart could stay
on the rails. Those gaberlunzies claimed to have hired
twice as many workers as they had, to pocket the
difference. Tashian found them out as they were
getting ready to flee with their loot."

"What did he do?"

"Chopped off their thieving heads, that's what. The
heads were still over the West Gate when Siggy and I
arrived. As you can imagine, this discouraged other
would-be railroaders; so at last His Excellence
appealed to Novorecife. We had just finished a job for
the Republic of Suruskand, so Kennedy recommends
us."

"I thought nobody who's had this new Saint-Rémy
treatment can teach Krishnans anything technical."

"We teach them nocht they don't already know. We
merely apply existing principles. The general idea of
bishtar-powered railroads either existed here when the
planet was first discovered or was divulged by one of
the first terrans to explore it, before the I. C. clamped
down. Somebody could get a Ph.D. thesis out of that
question. At the present rate of progress, though,
somebody's bound to invent a powered vehicle soon."

"Aren't you afraid for your heads?" asked Reith.

Strachan chuckled. "Kennedy made Tashy post a
muckle bond with Novo to assure our safe return. The

Regent bellowed a bit at the cost, but we wudna come otherwise. Anyway, we try to be reasonably honest. Bill Kennedy doesn't want any more mysterious disappearances, like that of Felix Borel."

"What happened to him?"

"We don't know. He came out to the end of the line and took off into the deep woods. Some Krishnan he'd swindled was after him. There's a rumor the Frenchie tried his tricks once too often, either on the self-styled Dasht of Zir or on the so-called Witch of Zir, but nobody knows. Mjipa wanted to drop a bomb to teach the beggars a lesson, as he put it. Percy's an able chap but a bit of an old-fashioned imperialist, and that's out of fashion." Strachan looked at Reith. "Come to think, Borel had red hair like yours."

"It's a wonder mine isn't gray, after what I've been through with my geese."

"Oh? Tell me your sorrowful tale." Strachan spoke in Durou to the servitor, ordering another round.

Reith narrated the adventures of his party at Gadri, at Majbur, and at Reshr. "After that, they calmed down pretty well. In Chesht that bleep Schwerin got in trouble again by taking pictures. Seems the Pandr of Lusht had granted a monopoly to some local photographer. This Krishnan used a camera like those of the first photographers on earth: a great big box on a tripod, and some sort of pollen sprinkled on a pan to make a flash.

"Then, while I was getting Otto out of this pickle, Valerie Mulroy, our resident nymphomaniac, was seducing an acolyte in the local temple of Kangand. I begged him off the flogging the priests were going to give him for breaking his vows; but then the poor fellow hanged himself in his cell. And Madame Jussac had some jewelry stolen, but she's a good sport—said it was only junk.

"Next, Valerie made a pitch for Guzmán-Vidal, and

77

I had a job to keep Señora Pilar from killing Valerie. In Uporé, Shirley Waterford, the black lady, almost started a riot by making a speech on the evils of racism to a crowd of tailed slaves. She'd found some broken-down, drunken old earthman to translate for her. She's a good-hearted soul, full of high ideals but with no common sense. To make it worse, Khorsh was off on some priestly errand, and I didn't know a word of Katai-Jhogorai. Some slave-owners tried to get up a mob to lynch us, but we got back to the ship before they got organized.

"Since then we've been on shipboard, and the weather's been too lousy to let them get into more mischief. Tell me, are there any terrans in Baianch besides Mjipa?"

"Couple of missionaries of terran cults, a con man or two, and a lady anthropologist who goes around measuring the Krishnans' heads. When they tell you all *Ertsuma* are daft, they cite her as their prime example. Right now, in addition, there's me, but I'm here for only a few days. I understand you and your people are coming out to Gha'id with me."

"Yes."

"Weel, I hope they don't mind really roughing it," said Strachan. "Out our way, everything bites, stings, or stinks, and anything nasty is twice as nasty as the corresponding terran pest."

"They've stood up pretty well so far," said Reith. "Old Mrs. Scott looks feeble, but she must be made of rubber bands and piano wires. But tell me about yourself, Ken. I've always wanted to see Scotland, where my folks came from."

"Aye? Let me tell you, it's not so romantical to one born and reared there. I come from Aberdeenshire, at the foot of the Grampians, and my one ambition was to get the hell out. You might say I'd succeeded better than anyone could have expected." Strachan took a big gulp, threw back his head, and sang:

> Barren are Caledonia's hills,
> Infertile are her plains.
> Bare-leggèd are her brawny nymphs,
> Bare-arsèd are her swains.

"Wait till you hear me play it on my bagpipes."

"Whose is that?" asked Reith.

"A Scot named Rennie, centuries back. He was an engineer, the same as I. In these degenerate days, of course, they're not bare-arsèd any more. When they wear the kilt, they put panties on underneath. I must get a local tailor to make me a kilt someday, if I can show him how. 'Tis no so simple as it looks." Strachan hiccuped. "How about a game of *piza*? Loser of two out of three pays for the drinks." He indicated the checkerboard pattern inlaid in the top of the little table on which they rested their mugs. "Just like Tashy, to charge his guests for the wee bit of liquor they drink."

"How do you play it?" asked Reith.

"I'll show you." Strachan took pieces out of a drawer in the table and set them on the table top. "First, a piece can move one square in any direction— forward, back, sideways, or diagonally...."

The game belonged to the family of checkerlike terran games, but with more pieces on a side than checkers and more complex rules about jumping and capturing. Strachan easily won the first game. Reith asked: "What was that about the self-styled Dasht of Zir and somebody called the Witch? Shouldn't I know about them?"

"Just a couple of local power-grabbers, out beyond the present end of the line. When we try to lay rails into Zir, there may be fireworks. That's one of my reasons for this visit. We heard that the Witch of Zir put a curse on the line, so half our workers quit. I had to come back to Baianch to recruit some more. Your first move this time."

On this occasion, Strachan barely nosed out Reith. "You catch on fast," he said. "I'd better quit while I'm ahead." He looked at the water clock against the wall. "Maun be going, laddie; I have a date for a good fuck. Would you want one, too? I can arrange it. Krishnan dames warm up faster than ours."

Reith hid his surprise. "I'd better not, thanks. I've got to be up early to keep my geese out of trouble."

"Weel, you know best; but don't let your moral standards worry you. The guid beuk forbids fornication with human beings and bestiality with sheep and other dumb brutes, but it says nocht about wimbling with extra-terrestrial hominoids. It's giving the terran preachers a hell of a time."

With a mug of Kvad still half full, Reith kept his seat while Strachan strode briskly off. Reith took out his notebook and ran over his list of the irregular verbs of Durou, while finishing his drink in leisurely fashion. Now that Khorsh had returned to his priestly duties in the temple of Bákh, Reith was oppressed by the need fully to master this exotic language without delay.

At last he paid up and rose to leave the New Palace. He found himself a little unsteady on his feet; he must have drunk more than he meant to. A man tried to keep up with Strachan in that activity at his peril.

He pulled himself together and set out for the entrance, walking with self-conscious precision. Mjipa's words about not letting the side down before extraterrestrials came to his mind. He had to make several turns and go through doors, where armored guardsmen stood impassively in pairs. They gave him only cursory glances.

He pushed through one pair of doors and recoiled in dismay. He found himself, not in the vestibule of the entrance as he expected, but in a sitting room. At a table, playing a game, sat Vázni and an older female Krishnan. Vázni gave a pleased squeal at the sight of Reith, who fumbled for the doorknob and stammered:

"I—so sorry—lost my ways."

"How fortunate!" cried the Douri. "Then you shall remain to entertain me, as a penance most condign for your mistake. Take a chair, good Master Reese!"

While Reith hesitated, Vázni spoke to her companion. The other Krishnan got up, bowed, said polite things, and departed.

Now Reith was truly appalled. From what he had read of terran history, he believed that, in a medieval court, to be caught alone with a royal female was enough to get a man shortened by a head. On the other hand, he was afraid openly to flout the princess's commands.

"Go on, sit you!" said Vázni. "At least, herein we need not shout to be heard above the uproar, as at today's party. Now tell me more of your far, exotical homeland!"

"I—I speak your language so bad—"

"Nonsense; 'twill give you good practice. I'll correct your errors. Do you take a single spouse apiece, or does each male wed a multitude of females, as among the heathen of Nich-Nyamadzë?"

Reith began a stumbling, laborious explanation of terran marital customs. By switching the subject to the rearing of children, he hoped to divert Vázni's mind from the form and functions of human genitalia.

As he spoke, Reith became aware of internal discomfort. As he knew, he had drunk more kvad than he usually allowed himself. Now this intake of liquid was having its effect. He had no idea of what to do.

What did one say on Krishna, especially to a princess? "May I wash my hands, please?" or "I've got to see a man about a dog?"

Such circumlocutions would only bewilder her, even if he could put them into Durou. Did these folk use such euphemisms, or did they come right out.... Squirming in his seat, he said:

"Highness, I beg you excuse me. Must see to my earthmen."

"Nay, linger a little while yet," she said. "Can I order a drink for you?"

"Thanks; I already have too much."

She looked sharply at him. "Sweat bedews your brow, good my sir. Find you the air too hot?"

"Nay, I—It just fine am," He gritted his teeth and tensed his sphincters. "Tell me, why do the Regent of richest Varasto kingdom dress so—so...." Reith tried to think of a Duro equivalent of "unpretentious."

She laughed. "Because my cousin, albeit the richest wight of the Triple Seas, is the most penurious. When I chide him for his beggarly raiment, he retorts that everyone in Dur knows him anyway, so where were the object of dressing up?"

"Better to err that way than other—to spend kingdom's money on show."

"For him, I ween 'tis his affair. What riles me is when he seeks the same regimen to impose on me. 'Tis said I'm not truly ugly; yet I might as well be, for the few wretched rags my beggarly clothing stipend allows me."

"I think you dress beautiful."

"Nay, flatterer; there's many a dame, wife of a merchant or even an artisan, better bedight than I. But now, I'd fain know more of the methods of begetting among the *Ertsuma*, whereof this afternoon you did begin to tell me. For ensample, what's the size and form of the organ male? And what confers upon it the necessary stiffness—why, Master Reese, find you that chair lacking in comfort? You fidget so. Here, take this one."

"No; it is not chair. I are not well. Must get back to my room for medicine." He started to rise.

"Alas, poor fellow! Is there aught I can—"

The door opened, and there stood the Regent, staring down from his nearly two hundred centimeters of height. In no friendly tone, Tashian said: "By Tyazan's nose, Master Reese! Little did I reck on finding you here."

Vázni burst into rapid speech. From the occasional word he caught, Reith inferred that she was explaining that he had merely lost his way, blundered into her quarters, and tried to withdraw, but she had detained him.

"I am sorry," said Reith, rising. "I should have ask guard the way, but my speech so bad is. Was just going."

Tashian looked the pair over narrowly. Although those flattish, semi-oriental Krishnan faces were not very expressive, Reith guessed that the Regent was weighing the facts that the two were seated across the table from each other, that their clothing was in order, and that Vázni could have called to the guards outside if Reith had attempted undue familiarities. Also, Reith thought, he doesn't want to spoil the tourist business in the bud. At last Tashian said:

"Well, Master Reese, we'll forget this trifling error. A Krishnan would not have paid such a lone nocturnal visit, but I believe your intent was innocent, and much can be excused a stranger."

"Your Excellency," said Reith desperately, "speak you any terran tongue?"

"A few words of Portuguese. Why?"

"Then please—*onde posso urinar*?"

Tashian's antennae twitched, as happened when

Krishnans were startled. Then he burst into a roar of laughter and smote Reith on the back. He almost knocked the smaller earthman down and, more importantly, nearly made him lose control of his abdominal muscles.

"So, that's what you were seeking! My good fellow, I'll show you straightaway. Off to bed with you, Vázni, ere you corrupt any more of our visitors from distant worlds. The stars give you a good night. Come with me, O Reese."

Following the Regent out, Reith reached up and gave his head a tug. He wanted to be sure it was firmly attached to him still.

VI.

THE RAILROAD TO ZIR

Considine and Turner climbed into the railroad car. Looking at the wooden seats, the former said:

"Hey, Fearless, what's this? A cattle car? I suppose you'd call it a shaihan car, eh?"

Silvester Pride grumbled: "These damned native shoes don't fit. The right and left are just alike. After I'd stood over the gook and showed him how I wanted them made, too!"

"Where will they put those workmen Mr. Strachan was hiring?" said Santiago Guzmán-Vidal. "We don't want a lot of essmelly natives in with us."

"Hae, laddie!" cried Strachan, swinging aboard. "All aboard the Gha'id Special?"

"All present," said Reith. "They're worried about the Duruma, though. They—ah—they'd rather not share the car—"

"What a bunch of bloody snobs!" said Strachan. "But they needn't worry. My Krishnans have two cars

85

of their own. They wouldn't want to ride with *Ertsuma* anyway; say they smell bad. There goes our other locomotive. We need a double-header."

The tourists looked out the window as the second bishtar lumbered past. The animal had a body and limbs of vaguely elephantine shape, save that six pillarlike legs supported the long, cylindrical body. Although furnished with a pair of trunks, the head was not like an elephant's. It more resembled that of a gigantic tapir, with an elongated, bifurcated proboscis. Each fork of the split trunk was about a meter long. The swiveling ears were of trumpetlike shape. The animal was covered with short, smooth, glossy fur, a deep purplish brown with white spots.

Abaft the ears, a Krishnan mahout sat on a saddle astride the neck, talking to the beast in a language known only to bishtars and their masters. From ahead came a rattle of chains as the second bishtar was harnessed in front of the first.

Then came another long wait, until the tourists squirmed and began asking Reith for explanations. Reith asked Strachan, who asked the conductor.

"Just stowing a piece of freight," reported Strachan.

"These natives!" said Guzmán-Vidal. "No sense of the time."

At last someone called: *"Byant-hao!"* A trumpet blew. The train started with a jerk and a clatter of couplings. It clicked over switch points and out on the qong-wood rails of the main line.

Flanges groaned, axles screeched, couplings clanked, and harness jingled. Under all the noise came the muffled thud of the twelve columnar legs of their power unit. Lurching and swaying, the twelve little wooden cars rolled westward at fourteen or fifteen terran kilometers an hour.

The track wound along the shore of the Va'andao Sea, of which those in the train caught occasional glimpses to the left. Otherwise an endless panorama of farm and forest swept past. After the first hour, the farms became scarcer.

Most of the time, the train was shut in on both sides by a dense temperate-zone forest. This, despite the rainbow hues of its foliage (like New Hampshire in the fall, said Mrs. Whitney Scott), in time became monotonous. Now and then, a wild Krishnan herbivore, grazing along the right of way, looked up from its nibbling and bolted into the woods as the train rocked past.

When the train began to descend a grade, whistles blew and trainmen shouted. These rushed back and forth to apply hand brakes, lest the cars roll forward and bump the after bishtar.

Turner got up to visit the little toilet enclosure in the end of the car. He grabbed at seat backs as the car lurched. At last he missed a grab and landed in the ample lap of Mélanie Jussac. Madame Jussac said:

"Oh, the little boy wants his mozzer, *non*? You are lucky you did not fall in the lap of the Señora Guzmán, or Santiago would be after you with his sword!"

Laughing, she set Turner back on his feet. He continued his lurching progress saying:

"This is worse than the old West Chester local, before they upgraded the roadbed."

After assuring himself that his tourists were safe for the nonce, Reith got up to explore. Forward, between their car and the two bishtars, were two flatcars piled with freight and lashed down with tarpaulins. Aft were two more coaches, filled with Krishnan workmen, and behind these came more freight cars. After a look at the meter-wide gap between his own swaying, yawing car and the next one aft, Reith went back into his own car and handed his sword to Guzmán-Vidal, saying:

"Would you please hold this, Santiago? I don't want

87

to jump to the next car and have this thing trip me up."

Reith jumped the gap and continued into the Krishnan-occupied car. He found Strachan on one of the seats, smoking a powerful Krishnan cigar and talking fluent Durou with one of his workmen.

"Ahoy, laddie!" said Strachan. "Not quite the Royal Scot, is it? But give 'em time. The Industrial Revolution's on its way. Come back in a hundred years and you won't know the planet. They'll probably go through an automobile age, the same as we did, until their petroleum gives out. That is, if they have petroleum."

"Won't that lead to a lot of turmoil, revolution, and so on?"

Strachan shrugged. "Belike, but what can we do? Once they know it can be done—and we've shown them it can by example—they'll not rest until they've done it, too. It does no good to warn them against terran mistakes. Still and on, they're an uncoly volatile, scrappy lot, so a little more violence won't make much difference."

"Ken," said Reith, "you were going to tell me about these characters out in Zir, the Dasht and the Witch." He had to shout to be heard above the clatter.

"Weel, now—hold on; we're going into a siding."

As the train struck a reverse curve, Reith grabbed a seat back to keep from being thrown into a Krishnan's lap. Trainmen bustled back and forth. Brake shoes ground, and the train slowed to a halt. They stood on a double-tracked section.

"What's this?" asked Reith.

"We're stopping for two purposes, namely, to wait for the regular eastbound daily from Jizorg to go by on the main track, and to eat our lunch."

"I wondered how we'd eat with these things bucking like broncos. Don't Krishnan railroads have double-tracked lines?"

"Not yet; traffic's not dense enough. Tell your folk to get off and stretch if they like. We shan't go off without them."

Reith hurried back to his own car and handed out the box lunches piled on one of the seats. Presently his tourists were all sitting or standing beside the train, eating and drinking. Up forward, the bishtars had been unhitched and guided to the edge of the forest. There they fell to feeding. Each animal grabbed a huge mass of many-colored vegetation in the fork of its cleft trunk, wrenched it loose, and stuffed it into its cavernous maw.

"Sheugh, man!" came a sudden shout from Strachan. "Watch that stuff!"

Reith looked around. Strachan was speaking to Professor Mulroy, who had been about to pick a sprig of a plant with leaves of a striking pattern of black and white stripes. Strachan explained:

"That's the *sha'pir*, or zebra weed if you prefer. It works like your American poison ivy. Only, in accord with the principle that everything nasty here is twice as nasty, it comes on twice as quick, itches twice as bad, and lasts twice as long.

"When Siggy and I were working in Suruskand, one hot day he took a dip in a pool in a river and then found he had nocht to dry himself with. So he tried to dry his hands, face, and other parts with these leaves. He was laid up so long that it cost us the bonus we'd have earned for finishing the job ahead of time."

"My word!" said the professor. "I am exceedingly grateful to you, Mr. Strachan. This plant looks interesting. It has evidently evolved a warning coloration, analogous to that of a terran hornet. I don't suppose there's a book on the poisonous plants of Krishna?"

"Not that I know. A couple of years ago, there was a human botanist in Suruskand, studying the plants. But the poor birkie went out without an escort once too often, and a yeki ate him."

"Dear me!" said Mulroy. Several tourists added exclamations. "I trust we shall not encounter such a pedator without adequate protection."

"Not here. The yeki is mainly a plains dweller, found in places like the prairies of Ruz. Here, the largest beast of prey is the yeki's smaller cousin the kargán, which seldom bothers game of our size. The most dangerous are the wild eshuna, which run in packs; but they avoid parties like ours."

"You relieve my apprehensions. I think I shall measure the bodily temperature of the bishtars." Mulroy produced a clinical thermometer. "I do not believe it has yet been ascertained."

"Hey!" said Reith. "If you try to stick that up its—"

"Have no fears, Fergus. That is not how one does it with a large, formidable animal."

"How, then?"

"It is simple. One follows the organism until it defecates and inserts the thermometer into a fresh dropping." The professor ambled off, expectantly watching the bishtars.

Having finished his lunch, Reith said in a low voice: "Ken, could you step over this way with me? I want to hear about Zir, but I'd rather my geese didn't overhear our talk."

"Weel, Fergus, Zir is a wild bit of mountainous country at the northwest corner of the Va'andao. Dur and Gozashtand both lay claim to it whiles, but neither can make its claim stick. The country's too rugged, and the Ziruma make things lively for outsiders."

"What about this fellow who calls himself lord of Zir?"

"Some years ago, Barré vas-Sarf got his start as a mere *bandido*, raiding the lowlands. Both Tashian and Eqrar have sent armies in after him, but they wore themselves out climbing mountain trails and were picked off in surprises and ambushes until they gave it up as a bad job.

"Meanwhile, Barré got more and more clans under his control, until he started calling himself the Dasht of Zir. Eqrar and Tashian have ordered him to declare fealty to them, but he's told them where to stuff their demands."

"And you think he'll let you run Tashian's railroad through his country?"

"Tashian thinks that, with the railroad, he can maintain enough soldiers at the end of the line to keep Barré from interfering. I hae ma doutes, but meanwhile Tashian's paying enough gold in at Novo to make it worth Siggy's and my while."

"How about the so-called Witch of Zir?"

Strachan laughed. "That's your God-damned missionaries. Why they let those maggot-mongers in, while they won't allow honest technicians like me to teach the Krishnans something useful, I dinna ken. Political influence in high places, I suppose. If they let in the Christians and Muslims and Buddhists and such, they have to admit all the daft little cults, too. Like that fellow we met in Suruskand, who went about telling the Krishnans they were the Ten Lost Tribes of Israel. He argued that, since a Krishnan animal called a *shomal* looks something like a camel, the names 'shomal' and 'camel' must come from the same root— some ancient Hebrew word, *gamal* I think.

"All this proselyting stirs up more violence and bloodshed than all the inventions of the Industrial Revolution put together. Anyhow, one of them converted a local priestess, years ago, and she built her own cult of his teachings. Now Shosti's the leader of a far-flung sect: the Ultimate Verity, I suppose you'd call it in English. She holds that the universe is the scene of a vast war between two hostile groups of interplanetary entities, the good and the bad. We *Ertsuma* are the bad. There's an unconfirmed rumor that the French swindler, Felix Borel, found refuge with her."

"But if he's one of the evil entities—"

"As I say, lad, it's not known if he went there or not. We've heard nocht direct since he disappeared into the mountains. Here comes the daily."

Another train, of five cars drawn by a single bishtar, appeared on the main track. Brave in red and blue paint, it rumbled past the sidetracked special. The Krishnans on the daily exchanged shouts and gestures of greeting with those waiting on the siding.

Strachan finished his fruit. "I see that Master Kherát, our gallant conductor, is gathering his men and beasts to move out. You'd best collect yours, too."

Reith got all his people back aboard the train save Otto Schwerin. A frantic search at last discovered Schwerin perched in a tree, photographing.

As yellow Roqir vanished behind the forested ridges, the special stopped on another siding at the village of Jizorg. Strachan led Reith and his tourists across the muddy main street to the inn. There a stout Krishnan quieted his eshun, which pulled on its chain and growled. This taverner then greeted the party with bows and voluble speech, too fast and in too strong a dialect for Reith to follow.

"He says," reported Strachan, "that in return for the honor of hosting the first tourist party from outer space, he's converting his hovel into a palace."

"Looks pretty much like a hovel still to me," said Considine.

In the courtyard, the taverner stopped at a well in the center. Two workmen were laying flat stones around the wellhead to form a terrace, while a Krishnan mason chipped another stone to make it fit the circular base of the wellhead. The taverner burst into speech, with gestures.

"He says," explained Strachan, "that the old well was good enough when he had only a few guests at a time; but, with the rise in traffic he foresees, the courtyard will be trampled into a sea of mud. Hence the masonry. Next, he says, he'll install a windlass and crank on the coping, instead of making the servants haul their buckets up hand over hand. I said the Industrial Revolution was on the way, did I no?"

Although Reith's tourists had become somewhat hardened, they were taken aback by the primitiveness of the accommodations. The fact that, with only four beds available, the men would have to sleep four in a bed caused especial complaint.

"I demand one bed for myself and my wife!" said Guzmán-Vidal. "The other four ladies can have the other bed. We never sleep apart, even when we are fighting!"

"Nothing doing," said Reith.

"But I am a *man*. I cannot be separated from my woman—"

"Do you want to go back to Novo on your own?" said Reith.

Guzmán-Vidal subsided, grumbling. When Pride and Considine in turn raised objections, Reith said:

"Now look here! You people set out on this very expensive and time-consuming tour because you wanted to see something different from earth, didn't you? You were warned you'd have to rough it, without terran amenities. If there were, you'd be like those people who want to go to Timbuktu, because the name sounds romantic. When they get there, they stay at the Timbuktu Hilton and complain it's like every other city. A little discomfort is the price you pay for anything really exotic."

• • •

A strange sound aroused Reith at sunrise. Looking out the window, he sighted Strachan, in his usual Krishnan costume, marching around the courtyard playing the bagpipes. Reith pulled on his clothes and went down to the yard, finding Strachan in a discussion with the taverner.

"One of my workmen disappeared during the night," Strachan explained. "Mine host here tells me this same Krishnan had passed through here going east a few days ago, stabled an aya with him, and took the train to Baianch. When our train arrived, this fellow came with the others. He just paid his stable charges and rode off."

"What's the catch?" asked Reith.

"The catch, laddie, is that he passed himself off as an ordinary construction worker and signed up with my crew, when he was evidently nocht of the sort. For one thing, a workman doesn't make enough siller to keep an aya. I think he's a spy, sent by Barré to report on the progress of the railroad."

"Does that put my people in danger?"

Strachan frowned. "Na, lad; I think not. At least, no more than they'd be in anyway, anywhere on this turbulent planet. Barré has no motive for molesting your folk. Besides, we're not that close to the border—if you can say there is a definite border.

"Anyway, Tashian has sent us a squad of lazy troopers to protect us. We asked for a company, but Tashy moaned about the expense." He shrugged. "It's in the hands of almighty Bákh, anyhow. You might say a prayer to him."

Reith hesitated. "Well—ah. . . ."

Strachan clapped Reith on the back. "Come on, Fergus ma boy! You'll be all right. I'll personally escort your people around, to see that they don't get into trouble. You'll be safer than you ever were on that ship, what with storms and pirates and a'."

"All right," said Reith. While on one hand he felt he was acting against his better judgment, on the other he was relieved to avoid the embarrassment of telling his tourists they had to turn back in the middle of their journey.

"Sall!" cried Strachan. "That's the spirit! I'll tell you. The Krishnans are all right; but a man gets damned tired of never having another terran to talk to. The Svensk is a good boss and a fine engineer, but he's as talkative as a gravestone. Time we were at breakfast, if we wullna hold up the train." He played a final run on his bagpipes and went in.

VII.

THE BANDIT KING

At Gha'id, Fergus Reith and his dozen climbed painfully down from their car. John Turner said:

"After three days in that thing, I feel like the little ball that whirls round and round in a cop's whistle. I wouldn't have believed anything moving so slowly could bounce around so."

Reith told his people to stay where they were while he went off to count the baggage. Further aft, Strachan was supervising the descent of his Krishnan workers. When Reith returned to his group, he found a tall, thin, dark-haired terran approaching.

"You are Mr. Reith?" said this one, extending a hand. "I am Sigvard Lund." The engineer spoke British English, with hardly a trace of the accent of his native Sweden. "If you will follow me, I shall show you to your accommodations. We had to build a quarter for you, since Gha'id has no inn. This way, be so good."

The "quarter" was a barrack of rough-hewn planks,

with four small rooms and one large one. The three married couples were assigned to three of the small compartments and Mrs. Whitney Scott and Shirley Waterford the remaining small one, while the rest of the men occupied bunks in the main room. There was a little excitement as the new arrivals disturbed some noxious-looking Krishnan scuttlers, but these were soon either stamped on or chased out.

After seeing his group and their baggage stowed, Reith told Strachan and Lund: "My people will need to rest tomorrow. The train trip sort of used them up."

"They are spoiled by terran luxury," said Lund austerely.

"Maybe so; but some are pretty old. Besides, they need time off to write letters and wash their socks."

The door of the engineers' sitting room opened. In came a young Krishnan in a Duro army uniform, with scarlet tunic, polished cuirass, winged helmet, and clanking sword.

"Fergus," said Strachan, "this is Gandubán vash-Sherdurogh, in command of our little guard. I suppose you'd call him about a third lieutenant." In Durou he said: "I present Master Fergus var-Reith, in command of the tourists."

Gandubán clicked heels, bowed, and shot out a hand. In barely comprehensible English, he said: "I is enchanted, good kind sir! I is honored! May you here stay happy be! I do anysing to help, wiz my brave men. I de good English speak, don't I not?"

Reith let his hand be wrung. When they were seated again, he resumed: "Then, the day after tomorrow, if you could get them out to the construction site, that should wrap it up. The next day, they'll be ready to leave."

Lund looked relieved. "You do not plan to remain longer?"

"No. They'll have seen all they want to."

"Excellent! I do not wish to appear inhospitable, Mr. Reith, and I am glad to see fellow-terrans from time to time. But your presence places a heavy responsibility on me, and your people are bound to delay our construction work. Even if you keep them from getting in the way, our workmen—many of whom have never seen an *Ertsu*—will stop work to gape.

"I shall order another special made up. We have an accumulation of empty goods wagons here, anyway, and it is time that some were returned to Baianch."

"Fine. When do we eat?"

"Soon. We should be glad to have you dine with us, but I suppose you are compelled to eat with your group?"

"On the contrary, Magic Carpet lets me eat away from them whenever possible."

"How so?"

"Look, if you had to listen to complaints and silly suggestions and hunt mislaid baggage and settle arguments all day long, wouldn't you want to get away from them?"

"Ah, I see. Very well, we shall be delighted. Kenneth, open the bottle, be so good."

Next morning, Reith watched as Gandubán drilled his twelve soldiers, in leather jacks studded with bronze buttons. They marched and counter-marched. They practiced swordsmanship, using nearby trees as pells. They shot arrows at butts.

When the guardsmen were dismissed, Gandubán approached Reith, crying: "Ah, de brave earsman! De explorer of strange worlds!"

Reith looked sharply to see if the Krishnan was being sarcastic, but nothing in Gandubán's tone or expression implied such a thing. Gandubán continued:

"I am great admire of earsmans. If you please, sir, I pray my English on you to practice. Already de good

Portuguese I speak: *Tamates! Graças a Deus! Va para o diablo!* So now I de English to learn must."

Reith replied in careful Durou: "I am sure, Master Gandubán, that my Durou is more in need of practice than your English."

"Okay, den, we some English, some Durou speak. Some day, earsmans all Krishna, as de earsmans call our world, will rule. Den de man who can speak good terran de good jobs get. I ready will be."

"Oh, come," said Reith. "You know the I. C. strictly forbids any sort of imperialism. The people at Novorecife may not interfere, even when our own people get into trouble—"

"Oh ho! You sink I simple am, believe dat? I read terran history, in de Brazilian mission school. I know. Nations wiz de best weapon, dey send spies who say dey be just missionaries, traders, scientists. Spies stir up trouble, give governments excuse to send soldiers. Pretty soon, backwards people all slaves of advance people. Happen over and over. Now it happen on Krishna, wiz people call demself missionary, scientist, now tourist." He winked at Reith, who had not before seen this gesture on Krishna. Gandubán must have learned it in the mission school. "But no worry. Gandubán—how you say?—land on him foots."

Reith argued but soon gave up, since Gandubán's conviction was not to be shaken. He traded language practice with the officer but was not sorry when the approach of lunch time gave him an excuse to go see to his tourists. Later, Strachan told him:

"I don't know how good a soldier Gandubán is, but he's too soapy by half. He'll kiss the arse of any terran who he thinks might have influence at Novo. If anyone was ever on the make, as you Yanks say, it's that young bladderskate. But that's these damned mission schools for you."

100

The morning of the day of leisure, Reith dropped in on Sigvard Lund, whom he found in his shed, working on a topographical map. Reith tried to engage Lund in conversation, hoping to pump him on the dangers of local travel. The tall Swede, however, proved as taciturn as Strachan was loquacious. Moreover, Lund indicated politely but firmly that he was a busy man without time for chit-chat.

Going out, Reith found Gandubán bustling up. "Mr. Reese!" cried the lieutenant. "What good chance! My mans is just dismiss. Now we practice de languages, not?"

The Krishnan attached himself to Reith with limpetlike adhesiveness. To make the best of the situation, Reith said:

"Tell me what you know about Barré vas-Sarf, please."

"Oh, dat big cliff!"

"Cliff? I don't—"

"You know; word mean place where land up steep go; also mean man who talk loud, don't nossing do."

"Oh, you mean bluff!"

"Yes, of course. See how value to me you is? Barré is just big bluff. Ride around, talk loud about stopping de railroad. Don't do nossing, really. Just bandit. My brave soldiers could chase away hundred times as many Ziruma. We no bluff! We real warriors!" Gandubán swept out his sword and made fencing motions. "You fence wiz sword?"

"I've had a little practice, but I'm sure you could cut my heart out on the first pass."

"Fine! We practice de fence, too! On guard!"

"Hey, not with real steel! Wait till I get my singlesticks. I'm out of practice."

"How clever!" said Gandubán when he saw the fencing masks and jackets. "You earsmans always do sings de right way. Dat why you rule my world some day. Now, on guard, my lord!"

A sweaty hour later, the Krishnan said: "You surprise; you good. Of course, you just beginning; I been doing for years. I ready for rest if you be. Come, we take shower bass."

The shower was a stall in which the bather stood, while his fellow climbed a ladder outside with a bucket of water. This he poured on a kind of grating or strainer over the bather's head.

When they stripped, Reith found Gandubán staring at Reith's person with an intentness that made Reith uneasy. Since, however, the Krishnan attempted no familiarities, Reith supposed it to be mere curiosity. Gandubán said:

"When Lund hear you coming, he make workers nail up dese curtains. Say many earsmen have funny idea about letting ozzers see dem wiz no clozes."

Reith yelled as icy water cascaded through the grating upon him. Dried and reclad, he asked in Durou:

"Now, pray, tell me about this Witch of Zir they speak of."

"Oh, that." Gandubán made a gesture of deprecation. "Will you, good my lord, flatter me by accepting this cigar?"

"Thank you, but nay. I smoke not. What about this witch?"

"Among the Ziruma there wafts about, like unto gossamer upon the morning's breeze, a wild, fantastic tale. Somewhere, they say, in the mountains dwells a sorceress immortal, attended by a retinue of imps and demons of incredible forms bizarre. Such is the beauty of this jade that no mere male against her can prevail. When one into her embraces is lured, instead of the

102

ecstasy the foolish wight anticipates, he is forthwith of certain parts and organs tragically bereft. These, the witch employs in composition of potions magical.

"The victim is then cast forth, alive but of only limited capacity. It is, I need not stress to one of Your Lordship's acuteness, mere superstition." Gandubán flicked an ash from his cigar. "None has upon one of these piteous mutilates set eyes. Even we poor backward Duruma are too sophisticated, such macaronic taradiddles to believe."

"Natheless," answered Reith, "the tale's not one to—to inspire confidence in him who guides so scatterbrained a flock as mine." Reith was feeling a little green from the smoke of the Krishnan's mighty cigar.

"Fear not, good my lord!" cried Gandubán. "With my gallant men and me to ward you, you'll be as safe as in the heart of Baianch fortress. We stand alert to shed our very lives, ere suffering a single hair of the earthfolks' hair to be harmed!"

At night, the bishtars were staked out in a line outside the camp. The line contained a score of the monsters. During the day, several were taken out to work on the construction site, while others were turned loose to forage.

"You've got to give them as much time eating as working," explained Strachan. "That pair that towed us from Baianch have done nocht but stuff themselves ever since. These four are for your folk."

Four bishtars had been led out of the line and now stood in a row, swaying from side to side. Krishnan workers lowered rope ladders from the howdahs and motioned Reith and his following to climb.

Mrs. Whitney Scott, to Reith's relief, had begged off. "I hate to miss anything," she said, "but at my age one sometimes has to."

That left Reith with eleven tourists. Strachan was going along to explain the sights. Gandubán and four of his soldiers were drawn up in a line, awaiting orders.

Each howdah contained six seats. Reith therefore divided his party among the bishtars, saying: "Will you take the lead animal, Ken, so you can tell us what we're coming to? I'll take the rear, to watch the rest. Lieutenant Gandubán, will you please put one soldier in each howdah and seat yourself on one of the middle animals?"

"Our valiant arms," said Gandubán in Durou, "shall be ever at Your Lordship's service."

When all were stowed, the leading mahout cried: "*Boí vegh!*" and blew a shrill little trumpet. His bishtar shuffled westward along the service road, which paralleled the rail line. The other three beasts followed. Although the howdahs rocked, the motion was easier than that of the rail car.

When they overtook a shaihan cart loaded with railroad ties, the bishtars had to crowd against the trees on one side of the road to get past the vehicle. Reith and his tourists fended off branches.

The road sloped up as they approached snow-capped Mount Kehar. Between the mountain and the sea, a ridge extended, rising to a point just before the slope plunged down into the Va'andao. Turning in his seat to call back, Strachan explained:

"The slope down to the water's too steep and rocky for us to put the rail line between yon peak and the sea, so we must go up over the saddle. It's a pretty problem. We have to branch off to the right, halfway round Mount Kehar, rising all the time, till we find a place flat enough to loop back and on up over the saddle. By the time we get down the other side, we shall have made an almost complete circle around the mountain."

"Why not go straight up over the pass?" asked a voice.

"Because the grade's too steep. We've got to keep the line below maximum grade, so the beasties can pull the cars up and the cars won't run away from us on the way down. The service road goes up this side of the pass by switchbacks, but a rail line canna make such sharp turns."

The service road forked, one branch going off to the right to follow the rail line and the other taking the shorter but steeper route up the pass. The party followed the left fork, which soon began to zigzag up the slope.

After several switchbacks, the group reached the construction site near the top of the pass. The rail line came in from the right, converging upon the service road.

First, the visitors came upon a crowd of Krishnan workers laying ties, spiking qong-wood rails down upon them, and shoveling gravel on the ties to ballast them.

Higher, another crowd was grading the right of way. A pair of bishtars, obeying the shouts of their mahouts, were clearing trees and brush. The larger trees they pushed over with their heads and dragged aside. The smaller trees and bushes they uprooted by wrapping both stubby trunks around the plant and heaving. A pile of brushwood crackled, sputtered, and sent up a cloud of blue smoke.

Another bishtar pulled a wheeled scraper blade to level the ground. Behind it, more workers shoveled dirt on the right of way and raked it level. Two more bishtars tramped back and forth to compact the soil.

Ahead of the grading area, a double line of stakes led off into the forest. Reith's bishtars followed the service road further, paralleling the stakes. Presently they caught up with more Krishnans and Sigvard Lund. The chief engineer was surveying the route with a simple instrument. This was a small plane table with plumb bobs for leveling and sights on top. Reith reflected that George Washington must have made his surveys with some such device. The Interplanetary Council forbade modern transits.

Lund looked up as the bishtars halted. "Is everything well, Mr. Reith?"

"Fine," said Reith. "Where would you like us to picnic?"

"Anywhere, so long as you do not get in the way." Lund returned to his instrument, checking the positions of the row of stakes, which extended off into the forest and out of sight. Reith called:

"Hey, Ken, there was a good view about two hundred meters back. Let's eat there."

The mahouts turned their animals and retraced their steps. Where a gap in the woods gave an open vista, they halted. The ladders were again unrolled and lowered, and the terrans descended.

To the east, the forested hills and patchwork farms of Dur spread out before them. Off to the right, the turquoise Va'andao Sea sparkled in the rays of Roqir. At the foot of the slope, the main railroad camp and the village of Gha'id looked like an ants' nest.

For the next hour, the travelers ate, slapped at small flying pests, and listened to Strachan lecturing on the details of Krishnan railroading. Lund came by, looked the party over, nodded silently, and strode on. Then Reith called:

"Okay, folks; time to go."

Gandubán shouted to the mahouts, who sat on their mounts while the bishtars stuffed greenery into their mouths. Presently, the four beasts were again lined up and the ladders emplaced. Strachan, who remained at the construction site, waved them off.

Soon the howdahs were swaying on the return

journey. Since it was downhill, they went faster than they had on the way up.

They had left the construction site behind when an uproar arose. Craning his neck, Reith saw a sudden movement among the workers. Screaming, the Krishnans ran off in all directions and disappeared in the woods.

A swarm of mounted men appeared on the service road, galloping after Reith's party. As they approached, Reith saw that they were wild-looking Krishnans wearing fur caps and bristling with weapons. They yelled and waved lances, lashing short-legged, scampering ayas.

Reith's mahout shouted *"Harzi! Harzi!"* The howdah's motion became violent. Ahead, the other bishtars had speeded up.

Although too heavy to trot or gallop, the animals could work up surprising speed by accelerating their shuffling walk. Nevertheless, the pursuers gained.

Reith looked at the soldier in his howdah, expecting to see preparations for a fight. Instead, the fellow cast his bow to the floor saying:

"We can do nought against fifty, sire. Needs must we be calm and pretend to be friendly."

Ahead, the other soldiers were doing likewise. Reith did not know whether to be angry at this poltroonery or to follow the advice. Before he could make up his mind, the convoy approached the first of the switchbacks.

"My God, Fearless!" quavered Silvester Pride. "At this speed, we'll never make the turn!"

The first bishtar leaned and skidded into the turn, almost made it, and slipped over the edge. As it disappeared, the second and third followed it.

Reith gripped the side of the howdah until his knuckles were white, wondering whether he should prepare to leap out. He heard his own voice squeak, uselessly addressing the mahout in English:

"Don't! You'll kill us!"

Shouting to his mount, the mahout paid no heed. The animal hesitated on the brink. Reith heard the rattle of loosened gravel. Then they pitched over, like the first dip on a roller coaster.

Amazed, Reith saw that all the bishtars had kept their feet, even on so steep a slope. Six legs were evidently better than four in such a case. The creatures slid spraddle-legged down the slope, sending an avalanche of stones and dirt ahead of them.

At the bottom, still going too fast to stop, the animals gallumped across the road and down the next slope. Since this one was gentler, they slowed enough to halt on the next switchback.

Behind, the pursuers were also taking the direct route. They slipped and slid, shouting *"Shtuí! Shtuí!"* This, Reith thought, must mean "halt" in the Ziro dialect.

The first bishtar started down the road but quickly pulled up. Barring the way, another crowd of Ziruma sat their ayas, arrows nocked and lances ready. The bishtars halted. The pursuing riders spread out, surrounding the bishtars, which stood panting with hanging heads. Reith estimated ninety or a hundred Ziruma.

A Ziru, better dressed than the rest, with a red scarf tied around his head, rode his aya out in front and called in Portuguese: *"Vocês! Descei!"*

The mahouts climbed from their saddles back into the howdahs and lowered the ladders. Reith called:

"He said to get down, people. We'd better do it."

Pilar Guzmán-Vidal was having hysterics, but her husband pushed and pulled her over the side of the howdah. Soon Reith, the tourists, the mahouts, and the five soldiers were lined up along the road. The well-dressed Krishnan walked up and down, looking over his quarry.

"This is an outrage!" said Considine. "I'll get the earthmen after you!"

The Krishnan leader looked blank. "*Não entendo. Quem fala Português?*"

"You mean he doesn't understand English?" said Valerie Mulroy. "All right, mister, you know something? You're full of shit, you son of a bitch!"

"Pipe down, both of you," said Reith. To the Ziru leader he said: "I speak some Portuguese and some Durou. Which do you prefer?"

"Are you the leader?" said the Krishnan in Durou.

"Aye, of these eleven *Ertsuma*."

"Are you the sightseeing travelers of who I have heard?"

"Aye. Are you Barré vas-Sarf?"

"Barré, Dasht of Zir, if you please. After all, I am who I am. How are you called?"

Reith gave his name. The Krishnan barked a command. Several of his followers dismounted, seized and disarmed the five soldiers, and began tying their wrists behind their backs.

When they sought to take Gandubán's sword, however, the officer suddenly whipped out the blade, ran the nearest Ziru through, broke away, and ran, leaving his sword in the Krishnan he had skewered. He leaped over the edge and went down the slope with giant strides.

The Ziruma set up a yell. Several shot at him. One arrow struck his back and bounced off his cuirass; another grazed his winged helmet. At a command, three riders spurred over the edge and started down the slope. Before they were halfway to the next switchback, however, Gandubán had reached the bottom, crossed the road, and disappeared into the forest.

Barré shouted; a trumpet blew a flourish. The three

109

pursuers halted and began walking their mounts back up along the road.

The leader stood looking down at the Ziru whom Gandubán had sworded. The Krishnan gave a shuddering breath and lay still.

Barré rattled out a string of commands in local dialect. A couple of his men took the swords away from Reith, Considine, Guzmán-Vidal, and Turner. Others pushed the four bound soldiers to the edge of the road and kicked them to make them kneel. A Ziru with an oversized sword came up behind one and swung. The blade struck home with a meaty sound. The soldier's head flew off and rolled down the slope. The body fell prone, lying half over the edge.

"I didn't know they had real blue blood!" said Turner.

"It is based on hemocyanin instead of hemoglobin," said Professor Mulroy. "That's why they have those greenish complexions. On earth, it is the oxygen-fixing compound in the blood of mollusks and arthropods. It's less efficient than hemoglobin, but Krishnan organisms have compensatory mechanisms."

The second soldier lost his head, and then the third. Blue-green blood bubbled, soaking into the loose soil of the bank below the road. Pilar Guzmán-Vidal and Shirley Waterford burst into tears.

"You mean," said Pride, "these folks are just a kind of glorified oysters? Then we could eat—"

"Shut up," snarled Reith, "or you may get the same treatment. I'm trying to listen."

The headsman was about to dispatch the fourth soldier when Barré said: *"Shtui!"* The Krishnan lowered his sword. The leader spoke to the four mahouts, who scrambled back upon their animals. The bishtars set out at a rapid shuffle on the road to the camp. The chieftain turned to the kneeling soldier and spoke in Durou:

110

"Are you fain to live, goodman?"

"Aye, sir," said the soldier faintly.

"Then I will enlarge you; but you must then carry out my command."

"Aye, my lord."

"You shall forthwith to your base camp proceed. I had hoped the two terran engineers to reave, but they all too nimbly did flee into the wold. When they return, you shall tell them I hold these other terrans for ransom. Any trickery—an attempt at rescue, for ensample—and they shall die instanter.

"On the morrow, I shall send an emissary to your construction site to present my terms. Should any try to seize his person, the hostages shall perish. If your masters fail to meet my envoy, I shall send him back the next day with a portion of a captive as an earnest, and another part the following day, and so on. Do you understand?"

"Aye, sire."

"Then cut him loose."

Freed of his bonds, the soldier rose stiffly and started down the road. Several Ziruma shouted jeers and insults. One drew an arrow and loosed, so that the missile whistled past the head of the soldier, who ducked and began to run. Barré stepped to the archer, struck him in the face, and made him follow the soldier to recover the arrow.

Considine said: "Some hero that Gandubán turned out to be! He talked big, but then he ran off and left us—"

"Keep quiet," said Reith. "He couldn't fight a hundred at once."

"All right," said Barré in Durou. "You earthmen shall come with us. If anyone attempt to flee, he may anticipate the fate of those imperialist hirelings. March!"

Reith translated. Herding the twelve captives, the

Ziruma set out up the switchback. One Ziru walked beside each prisoner, holding a wrist by a thong, while a mounted comrade led his aya.

Presently the party left the road for a forest trail, sloping upward. In despair, Reith plodded ahead, asking himself over and over where his big mistake had been. He tried to ignore the mutterings behind his back:

"It's all Fearless's fault."

"Sure. If he had any sense, he wouldn't have gotten us into this."

"Damn fool's obviously incompetent."

"He never listens to us."

"He should have left us at that *pueblo*, while he went ahead to esscout the country to see if it was safe."

"If I ever get out of this alive, I'll demand my money back."

The mutterings died away as the captives found they needed all their breath for climbing. Those who were overweight—the Jussacs, Shirley Waterford, and Silvester Pride—kept the rest of the party to a crawl, although prodded with lance points to speed them up.

Reith ruefully recalled his talk with Strachan at Jizorg. He had, he realized, let his own fear of loss of face before his tourists, together with the garrulous Scot's obvious hunger for human company, overrule his better judgment. It was small comfort to reflect that, if he had turned the group back to Baianch at Jizorg, they would have complained just as loudly. They would have grumbled over losing their money's worth because of his excessive caution.

VIII.

ARMS OF FLAME

When it seemed as though the older and stouter members of Reith's safari could go no further, the convoy came to a clearing. Here, more Ziruma guarded tethered ayas. The earthfolk were bundled aboard the stocky, six-legged beasts. Their wrists were attached by thongs to the horns on the fronts of the saddles, so that they had some freedom of movement but could not leave their mounts.

"For God's sake," said Reith, "don't fall off or you'll be dragged!"

"Don't I know it!" groaned Pride.

Ruddy beams from setting Roqir lanced horizontally through the close-set tree trunks when the party came out on another, larger clearing. Here were rows of tents and more armed Krishnans.

Barré vas-Sarf sprang down from his mount and shouted commands. Krishnans clustered around the tourists, untying their wrists and helping them down. Some could hardly move; several collapsed. Barré said:

"I regret the discomfort, good my sirs and madams; but my poor country affords no such luxe as does the imperialists' railroad. Be assured that you shall be entreated as guests during your stay. If you find your accommodations rude, they still surpass those that we poor fighters for freedom allow ourselves." He paused for Reith to translate, then went on: "Let us hope that my reasonable demands will be met, so that you shall soon be restored to liberty. My men will lead you to your quarters."

The quarters were a row of six tents in the middle of the encampment, with a clear space around them.

"They scared we've got something catching?" grumbled Considine.

"I think it's so they can watch us better," said Reith.

The couples, including Considine and Turner, each seized upon one tent. That left Reith, Pride, Schwerin, and Shirley Waterford with two unclaimed tents.

"I shall not share a tent with a man!" said Miss Waterford. "I'm a good Christian, and that's that."

"Then we'll have to split up one of the married pairs," said Reith.

"You don't essplit us up!" said Guzmán-Vidal. "A man with balls, like me—"

"We know all about your manhood," said Reith, "but—"

"Why don't we take the turn about?" said Aimé Jussac. "Even the brave Santiago can bear to be parted from his beautiful Pilar one night out of three."

"Okay," said Reith before the others could object. "That's how we'll do it. Professor Mulroy, will you bunk with me the first night?"

Mulroy nodded. Valerie Mulroy said: "Fearless, you know how Winston snores. If it keeps you awake, I'd be glad to change places—"

Reith interrupted: "Okay, everybody, they're lining up for chow. We'd better get in line, too."

He admitted to himself that, for all his neo-Puritan inhibitions, he would have liked a good roll in the hay. Valerie had not only broken him in but had also given him some expertise. But another liaison with her entailed more complications that he could cope with. Their peril was great enough without aggravating it.

"I don't think I can walk that far," groaned Pride; but, like the others, he limped and hobbled to the stew pots.

Reith found himself in the chow line between Considine and Turner. These began badgering him:

"Look, Fearless, you got us into this. Why don't you *do* something?"

"Yeah; these guys are liable to kill us."

"Maybe offer us as sacrifices to the great god Mumbo Jumbo."

"By slow torture."

"Or maybe barbecue us for supper."

"Yeah. Why don't you threaten 'em with the might of the terrans? We could blow them—"

"That's enough!" snapped Reith. "I'm doing what I can, and if you two raise a fuss, it'll just make my job harder. You were warned there'd be risk on this safari. I told you myself, at the briefing in Philadelphia. You're no more anxious to get out of here than I am, so don't hassle me." As Barré strolled past, Reith turned and spoke in Durou: "My lord! Do we not get plates to eat from, like unto the rest?"

"Certes!" said the chieftain. "I had forgot you bore no tableware when our hospitality was extended." A command brought a subordinate with a stack of wooden bowls and a fistful of horn spoons. Soon the hungry tourists' mouths were too full for complaints.

"Never thought I'd live to like this glop," sighed Turner, chewing a tough piece of unha meat.

"At least," said Considine, "it doesn't wriggle as you're eating it, like that live spaghetti they fed us at Jizorg."

Having taken a double-sized portion, Jussac said: "My little friends, you have the wrong attitude toward exotic foods. One should welcome them as part of one's gustatory experience. Me, I cherish the memory of every taste I have experienced on this planet, even when I found it horrible. To avoid such opportunities is like refusing to look at the buildings and monuments, for fear one might prove ugly."

"Okay for you, Aimé," growled Considine. "You always eat everything in sight anyway; and look at you, with that pod!"

Jussac patted his paunch. "But think of all my memories of beautiful meals!"

Reith hurried through his stew and took his spoon and bowl to the cask that served for dishwashing. The water did not seem to have been lately changed, so that tablewear washed in it came out hardly cleaner than when it went in. Reith cleaned his gear as best he could, wiping the implements with a handful of leaves. Then he sought out the place where Barré sat on a log, eating with his lieutenants.

"Sir!" said Reith. "Will you now have the goodness to explain—"

A burly Krishnan leaped up with an exclamation and whipped out his sword. Reith thought his time had come until the chieftain barked a command. The subordinate put away his weapon, and Barré explained:

"Fear not, Master Reese. My soldiers may not accost me without erst asking leave. Najjim here deemed you guilty of a breach of discipline. For you, howsomever, that rule shall not apply. What would you of me?"

"I do but wish to ask Your Excellence, wherefore you have distrained my party? Speak but slowly, I beg."

At least, that was what Reith thought he had said; but Barré looked puzzled.

"What said you?" asked the chieftain.

Reith repeated the sentence, articulating carefully and correcting errors of grammar and vocabulary.

"Oh," said Barré with a chuckle. "A transpicuous question, good my fellow." He waved an arm eastward. "Yonder lies the bloated, sprawling kingdom of Dur, in the avaricious grip of that straithanded niggard Tashian. Not satisfied with bleeding his own land dry to fill his bulging coffers, he casts his covetous eyes to uswards. He'd add our poor land of cliff and scaur to his possessions, to give his tax collectors another province to exploit. Well, we'll not endure it. Never shall the brave mountaineers of Zir bow to foreign yoke! Independence forever!"

"But what has that to do with my people?"

"Were numbers equal, never should we seek advantage of weaponry. One freedom-loving Ziru can rout three cowardly lowlanders. But numbers are not equal. For every man whom I can arm, Tashian can bring a dozen to the field. Therefore must we seek advantage by another path.

"Now, 'tis well known that you earthmen possess fell weapons, whereof any one makes our native armament appear as harmless as children's toys. You craftily keep them under lock at Novorecife, lest any be smuggled out and copied. One *Ertsu*, not long agone, seized the rule of Zamba and corruped one of Novo's petty bureaucrats to spirit him out a crate of these weapons, called 'arms of flame' or some such thing. But alas! a brace of *Ertso* agents, disguised as natives of this our world, did intercept the shipment and return it to their masters' control. The guilty official, I'm told, languishes in gyve and trammel even yet.

"So now, perchance, the headland does begin to loom through the fog of incomprehension? I have you and your fellows, and right gladly will I exchange you for a few cases of your arms of flame."

"How look you to accomplish that?" said Reith.

"I shall present my demand to Tashian, who will pass it on to Novorecife as speedily as can be. 'Tis in his interest to get this brabble settled, because of his ambition to make his land a favorite haunt of freely-spending terran travelers."

Reith said: "I think not that Novo will accede. They warn earthmen that, once outside the wall, they're on their own. If any be slain, that's regrettable but no cause for interference. So you're only harming your own interests by holding us."

"So? Well, we shall see if a hand or a head from one of your party, dissevered from its erstwhile owner, will not soften their severity. In any case, prepare yourselves for a lengthy sojourn; for 'twill consume at least a revolution of Sheb ere my message reach your fellow creatures and their answer be received."

A rainy spell kept Reith's tourists confined to their tents. There they became more cranky and quarrelsome than ever. When the rain passed, however, their spirits perked up.

Fergus Reith came out of his tent, where he had been calculating expenses, into the sunshine. His people were scattered about the camp, making the best of their circumstances. Shirley Waterford was trimming Silvester Pride's hair with borrowed shears, while Pride told her a long and dreary tale of what he called his rotten former marriage. Mélanie Jussac was washing the Jussac socks in the communal wash barrel. Professor Mulroy was peering through his pocket lens at a plant he had picked and writing notes. Several younger tourists were playing stick ball on the drill field to one side of the camp, using a headless spear shaft for the stick and a stuffed ball of native make.

Valerie Mulroy sat on a log with a Ziru, the burly junior officer who had almost sworded Reith for speaking to Barré without permission. She had begun to pick up a little of the local dialect. Now Valerie was practicing her new language on the Krishnan, who corrected her mistakes with loud laughter.

Otto Schwerin was sputtering indignant German at a group of Krishnans, who laughed at him. One of them had tried to disassemble one of Schwerin's cameras, using his knife as a screwdriver. Equipped with a self-destruct mechanism, the camera had exploded in a burst of cogwheels and other small parts. The Krishnan was holding his nose, which had been smartly struck by a lens.

"Mr. Reet!" shouted Schwerin. "*Diese barbarischen Einheimischen* my camera and one whole roll of film have ruin—"

Barré appeared among the tents, striding swiftly with a face like a thundercloud. Sighting Reith, he barked:

"Master Reese!"

"Aye, Your Excellence?"

"Come with me."

Reith gave Schwerin a sympathetic but noncommittal wave and followed the Ziru to the latter's tent, larger than those of the common soldiers but otherwise no fancier. A bronze lamp, hung from above, flickered and smoked.

"Sit down," said Barré. After a minute of glaring in silence, he said: "My emissary has returned from the rendezvous with Tashian's response."

"Well, sir?"

"He tells me Tashian spurns my proposal with scorn

and contumely. The losel claims he has no influence at Novorecife; and, moreover, he'll be damned to Hishkak before he'd provide me weapons wherewith to resist his righteous goal of reuniting his land."

"Reuniting?"

"The fact that a weak-kneed predecessor of mine once acknowledged Duro sovranty is used by him as a pretext, my submission to claim, notwithstanding that the Duro writ has not run in Zir for a generation." Barré sat seething silently for another minute, then added: "And furthermore, the *unha* added an insulting coda to his message, telling me where to stick my proposal. That is not a proper tone wherein one sovran should address another."

Barré, Reith thought, must be pretty naïve in worldly matters, despite his undoubted energy and qualities of leadership. Stumbling along in Durou and correcting himself, he said: "From what little I know of Krishnan politics, I think he is probably right about having no purchase at Novo."

"If I sent him a piece of one of you—"

"Excuse me, Your Excellency; but if he can't sway the earthmen, he can't, and sending him all our heads in a bag won't change matters. You'd just get Novorecife down on you as well."

"Think you he were moved by pity for you strangers to bestir himself?"

"I doubt if he knows what pity means. If you want to get a message to Novorecife, why not send a man the other way, by land through Gozashtand? It's shorter, if I remember the map."

"Because Eqrar's men so closely patrol the border zone that not a *burha* can slip through their net, and that little *zeft* is more hostile to Zir's independence than even Tashian."

Reith thought, then said: "There's one *Ertsu* in Baianch who might be able to help."

"Aye, sir? And who?"

"A man named Mjipa. He's there to set up a terran consulate. As an official of my own World Federation, he might have more effect than even the haughty Tashian."

Barré scowled. "A clever plan—but 'twere not practical. Never would Tashian suffer emissary of mine to travel to Baianch. His own subjects are forbidden contact with off-worlders save when commanded otherwise. From what his messenger told me, Tashian will obstruct any move towards fulfillment of my righteous aims."

A thought struck Reith. "Well, sir, you might send me as the envoy. Tashian could hardly object to my visiting a fellow earthman."

"Oho! Sits the wind in that quarter? But nay, my friend. I know somewhat about you *Ertsuma*. You're not so different from us, behind your ugly noses. Once your head be safely out of the yeki's mouth, you'll be in no haste to put it back in, as in the tale of King Sabzavar and the Gavehon thief.

"In fine, Master Reese, did I but let you go, you'd bolt for your terran stronghold, leaving your charges in the lurch. And thus should I relinquish my strongest piece in this game, to the boon of none but your crafty self."

"Oh, come, my lord! The first duty of a travelers' guide is to ward his people's safety. I take my task to heart."

Barré laughed and shook his head. "You're a plausible rascal; but what else would you say, good fellow, were you never so determined to flee these demesnes for ay? Nay, nay, 'tis useless to expostulate. Now if you'll excuse me—"

"Please, sir, one thing more. Who's this Shosti, whereof I hear? Is she on your side or the other?"

Barré gave a short, barking laugh. "*Ao!* The self-styled Priestess of Ultimate Verity holds a mountain stronghold northwest of here, clept Senarzé, whence she sends forth her influence maleficent. Whether 'tis in form of magical spells or merely fanatical followers, I wot not; but she gives me trouble enough for six. 'Tis she alone who blocks my holy purpose, the unity of Zir to forge, so that we shall stand united against all vile outsiders. I'll show you straight."

Barré opened a chest and took out a rolled-up map. He partly unrolled it. Then he looked sharply at Reith, rolled the parchment up again, and put it back in the chest.

"On second thoughts," he said, "I'd better not, I ween. One good look at yonder chart, and a clever earthman like you would have the picture of the lands and roads imprinted on his brain. 'Twere useful to you if you slipped away from us.

"To return to the drabby of Senarzé and her sect, I need a new religion, like unto hers, the support of my folk to solidify. That astrological cultus of Gozashtand pleases me not; all mathematics, without power to stir the emotions. From what I've heard, the Church of the Lords of Light sounds fitting for my purpose, but none of its missionaries has come to Dur. Doubtless they've been frightened off by the lies of Tashian and Eqrar, who make me out a bloody-handed barbarian instead of self-sacrificing patriot."

Reith said: "If I could arrange to fetch such a missionary hither, were it not a fair trade for your present captives?"

Barré chuckled. "Fertile in expedients, are you not? But nay; that were asking me to trade my sword for a spoon. Both have their utility, but that makes them not equal in value. Moreover, much as I should like this missionary whereof you speak, I'll not let you go wandering abroad on your promise to enlist one. Did you offer a certain means of bringing the accursed

Witch within my governance, now, that were different."

"Might one say that Shosti stands in the same relation to you that you do to Tashian?"

"*Fointsaq*, no! 'Tis a different affair entirely. That's unkind of you, Master Reese, after I've striven to entreat you and yours as sweetly as our mountain poverty and the exigencies of the case permit. You have my leave to go."

Reith left Barré still sputtering his indignation. Out in the light of Roqir again, he walked, deep in thought. A good look at that map would have been useful.

Reith wondered at his chances of getting into Barré's tent and sneaking a look at the map in the chieftain's absence. But no, that seemed unlikely. There were always at least a couple of Ziruma guarding the tent; Barré was not slack in running his army. Reith's own maps were back in Gha'id, and anyway none showed Zir in enough detail.

Reith wandered past the place where Valerie Mulroy continued her language lesson with Captain Najjim. They paid Reith no heed. Valerie was looking at the Krishnan with an expression Reith recognized; he was not surprised to hear her say:

". . . . in the midnights."

"At midnight, you mean," said Najjim. "'Twill do most excellently. I have the guard tonight. I'll meet you on the south side of camp, having sent the other sentries to the other sides. Agreed?"

Reith, still thinking, passed out of earshot. He had no definite idea of where the camp was, other than that it lay somewhere west of Gha'id and the railroad construction site. They were near the top of a large hill or small mountain, but the surrounding forest hemmed in the vista.

"Hey, Fearless!" shouted Maurice Considine, who

was acting as catcher. "Come and take a turn at bat."

Reith had not swung a bat at a ball in years, but he joined the game. Considine said:

"We use those two stumps and that old dead tree as bases."

Reith struck out and endured the others' gibes at his clumsiness. On his next turn, however, he hit a homer. When he got back to the home plate, he murmured to Considine:

"Maurice! Pretend to quarrel with me and chase me up that tree."

"What? Why?"

"Never mind why! Just do it."

Considine puzzled briefly, then fell into the spirit of Reith's proposal. He shouted:

"Hey, that's not fair! Fearless didn't touch the second stump!"

"I did, too!" cried Reith.

"Are you calling me a liar?"

"You're damned right! I kicked that stump as plain as anything. I'd have broken a toe if I'd kicked it any harder."

"I don't let any skinny, red-haired son of a bitch call me a liar! You take that back, or I'll push your teeth down your throat!"

Aimé Jussac came puffing up. "Boys! Boys! Do not quarrel in the face of the enemy!"

Reith and Considine each made a couple of wild swings, missing the other by half a meter. Then Reith ran to the dead tree, with Considine behind him, and swarmed up into the branches. Considine climbed after him. The two Krishnans guarding the prisoners looked on, showing amusement at the antics of off-worlders.

Higher and higher went Fergus Reith, until he reached the canopy level of the surrounding forest. As the intervening foliage fell away, he found himself looking across the lower peaks and ridges to snow-capped Mount Kehar. There was no mistaking that looming mass. The smaller but sharper peak rose south of it, on the edge of the sea and connected with the mountain by a saddle-shaped ridge.

"Come down at once, you!" shouted a Krishnan voice.

Reith looked down to see Captain Najjim standing below.

"Go on down, Maurice," said Reith.

When Considine was out of the way, Reith took a last look at the landscape, trying to memorize every bump and hollow. Then he descended. Considine was trying to explain in his few words of Durou that he and Reith had been just horsing around. The phrase came out in Durou as "making ayas," which left Najjim baffled.

"He means, we did but jest," said Reith. "We are friends in spite of all."

"You *Ertsuma* must be stark mad," said Captain Najjim. "Do such japeries no more!"

"Aye, gallant captain," said Reith. To Considine he added: "Maurice, don't you know that *aya* has an irregular plural?"

Considine waited until Najjim had stalked off. Then he asked: "What's this all about, Fearless?"

"I wanted a look at the country round about, just in case; and I needed an excuse to climb that tree."

"Oh? I see! You're thinking of es—"

"Sh! Don't say that word. Don't discuss it, either. Some blabbermouth would let the cat out of the bag. If I disappear, it won't be just to save my own skin, but because I think it's the best way to spring the rest of you."

"Well, look, why can't you take me and John, too? We're younger and huskier than the others. We could—"

"No; this is best done alone. Besides, you two are needed here."

* * *

125

That night, Reith shared his tent with Aimé Jussac. At bedtime, he confided his intention of escaping to the Frenchman.

"Ah! *Magnifique!*" said Jussac. "If I were not so old and fat, I would essay something like that."

"Someone," Reith continued, "will have to be left in command. I think you're the man. You seem to have your head screwed on tighter than most."

"You do me honor, my friend. But, if I may offer a suggestion, I shall tell them merely that you have nominated me for the post, or made me provisional leader until I can hold an election. A leader who is freely elected will command the loyalty of the others better than one who is merely appointed."

"Okay, any way you like. Didn't I hear you talking Durou to one of the Krishnans?"

Jussac shrugged. "I have picked up a smattering. I already speak six languages, so one more has presented no great difficulty."

"Good. Now, if you'll go to sleep and snore good and loud...."

Jussac blew out the lamp. From the dark came sounds of his composing himself to sleep. Reith crouched at the front of the tent, peering through the crack between the flaps.

Outside, beyond Reith's range of vision, sentries paced and exchanged passwords. Kairrim, the largest of the three satellites, flooded the camp site with silvery light, thrice as strong as that of the terran moon. Something howled in the distance.

After a long wait, faint sound and motion alerted Reith. A shadowy form, which he recognized as that of Valerie Mulroy, drifted past his tent. At first he thought she was on her way to the latrine. Then she went off to southward to her rendezvous.

Reith picked up the sack of biscuits that he had, with Considine's help, purloined at supper. He stole out and, crouching, moved south on Valerie's trail, keeping her barely in sight.

A quarter-hour later, he had reached the woods south of the camp. The polychrome of the Krishnan foliage had faded in the moonlight to a uniform silver.

Confident that no sentries would be here except Najjim, whose mind would be on other matters, Reith entered the forest. He felt each step before putting his foot down, lest he make a dry twig snap.

Faint sounds came from his right. He heard a giggle and words in Valerie's voice, and then Najjim's deeper tones.

Reith detoured to the left to be sure of missing the amorous pair. Straining his eyes, he picked out motion to his right. Splotched with moonlight, something long and dark lay on the ground among the tree trunks. The form humped itself up in the middle, sank down again, and continued rhythmically rising and falling.

Reith tightened his lips to suppress a chuckle. Knowing Valerie's capacities, he suspected that she would wear down even the lusty captain. In any case, she would give him a memorable ride.

Keeping Karrim on his right, Reith felt his way through the trees. Away from the camp, the underbrush thinned so that he could move more easily. He tried to remember the topography between the camp and Mount Kehar, as he had seen it from the tree....

Then a hairy hand was clapped over his mouth from behind, while other hands seized the limbs. The hand over his mouth was withdrawn; but, when he filled his lungs to yell, a gag was stuffed into his mouth.

In a few minutes, he was hog-tied and slung by wrists and ankles from a carrying pole. His captors, as nearly as he could make out in the uncertain light, were tailed Krishnans of the kind he had seen employed as slaves. Their main independent settlement near Novorecife was in the Koloft Swamp, and in most of

127

the Varasto languages they were called Koloftuma.

The Koloftuma set briskly out. The pole whence Reith dangled was carried on the shoulders of two, while several others trotted ahead and behind.

If Reith had found his ride on aya-back, from Mount Kehar to Barré's camp, uncomfortable, it was the height of comfort compared to this torture. But his captors trotted tirelessly on, paying no heed to his grunts, groans, and gurgles.

IX.

THE GOLDEN SKULL

Eons of pain later, Fergus Reith was borne to a
clearing. There others, some with lanterns, waited.
Since Karrim had set, Reith could not tell much about
these others. From size and sound, he guessed them to
be ordinary tailless Krishnans.

The tailed Krishnans talked with the new group, but
the dialect passed Reith's understanding. The Koloftuma lowered Reith, cut his bonds, and ungagged him.
Others helped him to his feet and supported him while
life returned to his tortured limbs.

When he could stand unaided, Reith was amazed
when, at a signal, the Krishnans around him knelt
down. One said in Durou:

"Hail, Your serene Divinity!"

"Who, me?" said Reith. Some Krishnans were
leading ayas into the clearing.

"Aye, Your Divinity. We have come to take you to
our mistress, the divine Protectress. Be so good as to

129

mount and ride with us. Pray, essay not to flee, for the Koloftuma can track you with ease."

"If I be so divine," said Reith, "why are you using force with me?"

"All shall be made clear, when we shall have brought you to Her Rectitude. Kindly mount this beast."

Reith considered a break for liberty but decided against it. In his present state, they could catch him before he had gone three steps. Wincing, he climbed into the saddle. A Krishnan on another mount held Reith's reins, braided into the aya's mustache.

Although Reith had had scant experience with horses, he wished that he had one now instead of this horned, six-legged monstrosity. The saddle was mounted over the middle pair of legs, so that the shock of each footfall was transmitted directly to the rider. Not even the heavily-padded Krishnan saddle did much to cushion the jar.

Roqir was rising in scarlet and vermilion glory when the cavalcade wound up a steep-sided vale between rocky cliffs and barren hills. The slope became steeper. Reith sighted a cluster of structures atop a crag, standing almost isolated from the surrounding mountains but joined to the nearest by a narrow saddle.

The trail wound up to this ridge, between a vertical cliff on one side and a sheer drop of hundreds of meters on the other. Reith shut his eyes as they ambled past the worst places, hoping that his mount's six legs would provide the needed margin of safety.

As they neared the stronghold of the Witch of Zir, the yellow sun flashed from the gilding on the central tower of the main structure. Rainbow-hued prismatic beams shot from a large, faceted glass ornament surmounting this tower. This building, thought Reith, must be the temple.

Lower buildings of mortared gray fieldstone surrounded the temple, their lower parts hidden behind a massive wall. The dark wall and low buildings contrasted with the marblelike cream color of the tower. The impression was of provincial crudity surrounding a center of barbaric magnificence.

"Behold Senarzé, the spiritual center of this mundane world!" said the leader of the Ziruma.

They trotted out upon the narrow ridge that joined the stronghold to the neighboring heights. As they neared the place, a drawbridge came down with a rattle of chains and a thump. Reith saw that the rock had been dug away beneath the drawbridge, forming a ditch across the ridge. Hence, when the drawbridge was up, the stronghold was impregnable unless the attackers could scale the surrounding cliffs. This would be a mountaineering feat, involving the use of ropes and pitons, even if nobody were dropping things upon the climber.

They clattered over the drawbridge, beneath the portcullis, and through massive gates of squared timbers with bronze fittings. Inside, the Krishnans drew up and dismounted in a small square, surrounded by houses of three and four stories.

Other Krishnans, many in armor, awaited them. The armor, like that of the other Varasto nations, had a Moorish look, having many small plates connected by stretches of chain mail. Behind them, winches clattered and chains jangled as the drawbridge was raised again.

Reith's captors bowed and spoke to a hooded figure, shorter than the others, whom Reith took from the cut of its cloak to be a Krishnan female.

"Pray dismount, divine sir!" said the captor who

had spoken to Reith before.

Reith stifled a groan as he swung down. He staggered, caught the saddle, and steadied himself.

"Turn," said the cloaked woman.

Reith did a double about-face. The woman spoke to the commander of the party. Reith thought she said: "It is indeed he!" in the Ziro dialect. She gave another order.

"Pray come with me, Your Divinity," said the commander.

Four other Krishnans closed in about Reith, who could not see any reason for these precautions. Now that the drawbridge was up, there was no way out of the stronghold.

The procession marched up the steps of the temple, the gleaming façade of which was ornamented with patterns of semi-precious stones. Reliefs of gods and goddesses in stiffly dignified attitudes stared down. A few early-rising Senarzeva, going about their business, glanced curiously at Reith and his escort.

Inside the huge bronze doors, Reith was led through halls and passages to a group of secluded chambers. When they halted in a large bed-sitting room lit by two golden candelabra, the leader of the escort said:

"Pray be seated, divine sir! Take your ease! All shall be done for your comfort."

Reith sat. Turning in his chair, he asked: "Why am I here? What wants Shosti of me?"

"I beg that Your Divinity have patience," said the leader. "All shall be explained."

All but the leader and one other Ziru departed. These two stood before the door by which they had entered, watching Reith.

Another door opened. In came a squad of young females in gauzy draperies. They knelt before Reith and bowed to the floor. They chattered girlishly at him, but only one spoke standard Durou. She said:

"Suffer us to minister to Your Divinity, my lord!"

The next thing Reith knew, they were unbuttoning his clothing.

"Hey!" said Reith. "What—"

"Your serene Divinity will wish his bath, will he not?" said the Durou-speaker. "Pray, how works this thing?" She was struggling with a zipper.

"If you will tell me why I am here and what you plan to do with me, I will show you."

They went off into shrieking giggles. "Pray excuse us, Your Divinity. That is for our Protectress alone to tell you."

Reith sighed and gave up. Before his capture by Barré, he had begun to think of himself as a man of action, a master of his own and others' fates. Ever since then he had been reduced, step by step, to impotence. Physically and emotionally exhausted, he felt like a bug tossed on a chip on the sea of life. Although he still worried about his tourists, there was nothing he could do for them at the moment.

He helped the girl with the zipper. Docilely, he let them strip him and lead him into a bathroom.

The bronze tub, thought Reith, was big enough to bathe a bishtar. He got into it by a stepladder. The girls discarded their gauze and set about washing him. The Durou-speaker produced a flat cake of brown substance, wet it, rubbed it with a washrag, and applied the rag to Reith's back. Good God, he thought, this looks like real soap!

"What is your name?" he asked the girl.

"Beizi."

"What is that stuff, O Beizi?"

"Oh, my lord, this is a piece of magical essence, which one of the first of you creatures from outer space brought with him. It has been in the Protectress's family for generations. 'Tis used only on special occasions, lest it all be dissolved away. Our Protectress

133

sees fit to honor Your Divinity by the use of this stuff, called *savunit* or something."

Reith recognized the Portuguese word for soap, *sabonête.* He was fairly inured to Krishnan bath customs. Nevertheless, the presence of these attendants, unmistakably female despite their alienness, put ideas in his head of which he would not, in his present fatigue, have thought himself capable. One bent over to scrub him, her breast gently rubbing back and forth against his shoulder. He crouched down to hide the physical evidence of his thoughts.

By mentally running over the irregular verbs of Durou, Reith at last persuaded the manifestation to subside. When he stood up to be dried, there was a burst of chatter among the girls. Beizi explained:

"You *Ertsuma* have such a funny shape, all dangly. It must expose you to injury. . . ."

"Never mind my shape," said Reith. "Just fetch my clothes, if you please."

"Oh, but my lord, you must not wear those dirty, ragged old things again! You shall be arrayed as befits your divinity."

"What have you done with my old clothes?"

"N-nought, Your Divinity. If you are fain to keep them in memory of your journey hither, we will mend and wash them."

They took Reith back to the bedroom. While one girl sewed a rent in Reith's shirt, the others clad him in an outfit as glittering as that of any old-time oriental potentate. The outer garments were cloth-of-gold trousers, tunic, and turban. A jeweled bangle was affixed to the front of the turban. Over the tunic, Reith wore a scarlet sash studded with emeralds.

Very pretty, Reith thought as he surveyed himself in the mirror. He would have preferred his own plain garb; where in hell were any pockets? He tried to explain about pockets but found he could not speak the needed words.

"Hand me my pants and jacket." he said.

When this was done, he demonstrated the pockets. "I need them to carry my little things—wallet, knife, comb, pen, and so on."

"How quaint!" said Beizi, giggling. "Here, you tuck those things into your girdle."

"I still want these—these little bags in my clothes. Can you girls make them?"

"We will try. Your Divinity's slightest wish is law—provided of course that you attempt not to leave Senarzé. Now my lord must be hungry."

"Famished, young lady; also sleepy."

An hour later, Fergus Reith, full of the best breakfast he had eaten on Krishna, was sound asleep in the bed furnished by Shosti, Protectress of the Temple of Ultimate Verity at Senarzé.

When Reith awoke, the direction of a ruddy sunbeam through a narrow window told him that Roqir neared the horizon. In came the same squad of attendants. Beizi said:

"We have been peeping in on you for an hour, my lord. Permit us to clothe Your Divinity and lead you to our Protectress."

Reith felt his bristly chin. "I must—ah—how say you?—cut face fair first?"

"Oh? I have heard that male *Ertsuma* grow hair all over their faces, but I have never seen one close. Suffer me to look, my lord."

She touched Reith's chin and jerked her finger back with a yelp. "It prickles! How do you this cutting?"

"I'll show you. Fetch a basin of warm water and some of that *savunit*."

They watched him, squealing with delight, as he

scraped his face with the small razor in his pocket case. Although beards had again been in fashion when Reith left the earth, he and his male tourists were clean-shaven in deference to the prejudices of the nearly beardless Krishnans.

When he was again arrayed in splendor, Reith was led through rooms and halls to a chamber where a Krishnan woman sat, in gauzy garments of cobalt blue, like those of the attendants, but with a jeweled tiara on her greenish-black hair. She rose and bowed.

"I am Shosti, Your Divinity," she said. "Do I understand that your mortal name is Reese?"

"That is close enough," said Reith. "Now, madam, kindly tell me why you have kidnapped me and what this divinity stuff is all about."

"You shall hear in due course, my lord. Pray sit."

Now that he had a better look at the Witch of Zir, Reith took her to be a good deal older than her handmaidens. She was fairly good-looking, as Krishnans went, but nothing out of the ordinary. It was hard to tell Krishnans' ages, since their flattish, oriental-looking faces did not wrinkle much.

Moreover, the life spans of the two species differed. That of Krishnans was intermediate between that of a normal, unmedicated earthman and that of an earthman who regularly took longevity pills. Reith and his tourists were well supplied with these medicaments.

"Will you soon be boun for another repast, my lord?" said Shosti.

"Aye, my lady. But if you will explain—"

"In good time, I pray. Fetch some kvad, Beizi, and tell the cook to lay on dinner."

When the liquor had been brought, she said: "I am told, my lord, that before taking the first drink, earthmen raise their glasses and say 'To your health!' to each other. Be that true?"

"Aye, madam. Nearly all our languages have a

phrase for it: *à votre santé, à sua saúde,* and so on."

"Then, to your health, Your serene Divinity!" She performed the gesture awkwardly.

Reith took a sip. "Now, madam—"

"I am coming to that. Know you the prophecies of Gámand the Unshorn?"

"I fear not."

"Gámand lived around the end of the Kalwm Empire. His prophecies were indited by his acolytes, but during the Dark Age, many sheets were lost and the rest became jumbled. Hence we must needs interpret them in the light of events. When something strange takes place, we look in the prophecies of Gámand and say, why, here the event is plainly foretold! But, what with the archaism of the language and the confusion of the order of the texts, we could not anticipate the event in time to forestall it.

"Now, prophecy number one hundred and forty-three says that a god shall appear in an unearthly form, with hair of flame. Upon the mistress of the spire he shall beget an heroic demigod, who shall free the people of the world from unjust, oppressive rulers and launch an era of peace, joy, and prosperity."

"What has that to do with me?"

"Your Divinity does but jest; for surely your all-knowing mind can see that the god with flaming hair is yourself."

"Who, me?"

"Aye, divine sir. And the pinchfist is that grasping niggard Tashian. The mistress of the spire is my humble self; for the spire is plainly this peak of Senarzé, whereon the Temple of Ultimate Verity stands. What chance, think you, that these things would fit the prophecy by mere happenstance?"

Reith gulped. "You mean you expect me to—ah—beget this demigod? Here and now?"

"Certes, good my lord; or rather, after we have

enjoyed a good repast. You understand, of course, that the prophecy concerning you could not be grasped in its full import until the missionaries of Ultimate Verity enlightened us about the cosmic conflict, raging through the universe, between the gods of light and the gods of darkness. Your hair proves you one of the gods of light; for, when a god assumes a mortal guise, he cannot hide all the stigmata of his divinity. Have some more kvad."

"Gramercy," said Reith, taking a deep pull. "But, you know, earthmen and Krishnans. . . ."

"Eh? What's that, Your Divinity?"

Reith was going to explain that hybridization of species from different worlds, no matter how superficially alike, was a biological impossibility. On second thought, he decided to say nothing for the present. If he made a point of their mutual sterility, Shosti might find his presence an embarrassment and have him pitched off the cliff. He finished lamely:

"Nought, madam. I did but hope that—ah—the key would fit the lock."

"Fear not, my lord. I have made trial of you *Ertsuma* before and find them compatible. Ah, here's dinner."

As a paling sky presaged the rise of Roqir, Fergus Reith yawned and sat up in the huge bed. Shosti slept soundly. As he lowered his feet to the floor and felt for his slippers, he looked at her with a slight grimace of distaste. Shosti was a well-built female, attractive by either terran or Krishnan standards, but she appeared to have no interest in sex as such. She had submitted passively, evidently viewing this contact as a religious duty and not as an occasion for pleasure. There was no romance about it—not even so much as in his liaison with Valerie Mulroy on the *Goyaz*. Reith was left feeling like a hired stud.

Although Reith did not often let his neo-Puritan upbringing get in his way, he harbored a romantic yearning to find a dream girl and carry her off forever. So far from being romantic, copulating with Shosti was just a piece of exobiological research. Professor Mulroy would be interested, if Reith survived to tell him about it. He remembered the limerick he had heard from Santiago Guzmán-Vidal:

> There was an old gaucho named Bruno,
> Who said: "Sex is one thing I do know.
>   A woman is fine,
>   But a sheep is divine,
> And a llama—(smack)—*numero uno*!"

Where, he wondered, would Bruno have placed female Krishnans on his scale?

Reith eased himself off the bed and wrapped himself in a gauzy, frilly nightrobe. He looked down at the garment in disgust, thinking it would suit the dear boys better than him.

As he tiptoed towards the door, a golden gleam caught his eye. On a shelf above the lintel stood a golden skull. The previous night, between lust and dim lighting, he had not noticed it.

He reached up and touched the object. It was far too light to be solid gold. He lifted it down between his finger tips.

It was either the gilded skull of an earthman or a marvelous imitation. Although Reith was no osteologist, he knew enough about terran and Krishnan anatomy to be sure that this was a human skull. The jawbone had been secured to the skull by golden wires.

Reith replaced the skull, stole out, and returned to his bedroom. None of the girlish attendants was there.

When he had attended to his most immediate need, he looked around for means of summoning his tiring women.

A rope came through a hole in the wall, near the ceiling, and hung down within easy reach. Reith pulled. Somewhere a bell jangled. An instant later, two of the girls entered, squeaking.

"God den, mortal maidens," he said in an attempt at the Ziro dialect. "Fetch Beizi, if you please. Meanwhile, kindly dress me."

When Beizi arrived, she burst out: "The Protectress is awake. Her Rectitude was pleased with your performance last night."

"Kind of her, but she controlled her enthusiasm," said Reith.

"For her, my lord, it is a serious spiritual duty, not an occasion for frivolous pleasure. Natheless, she's fain to couple with you every night, until she knows herself gravid."

"That's flattering, but I fear the mortal body wherein I am incarnate needs a night off betimes."

The girls looked downcast, murmuring. Beizi explained: "We had hoped Your Divinity might have some divine seed left for us."

"For shame, Beizi!" said another girl. "You should not make such scandalous suggestions, even in jest."

"I jested not," said Beizi. "Whereas we're forbidden commerce with males, such restrictions would not apply to His Divinity. Would they now, my lord?"

Reith replied: "When I have my sacred duty performed and gotten Shosti pregnant, we shall see. But how will she know? Terran woman have a simple indication, but you Krishnans are different."

"She will suddenly lose all her sexual lust within a few days of conception."

"I thought she had none to lose?" said Reith.

"She does a little, however sternly she curbs it. With

pregnancy, the mere thought of coition becomes repugnant. No Krishnan woman could mistake the feeling."

"I see. Should I join Her Rectitude for breakfast?"

"Nay, my lord. She sends her regrets; but for the next hour, the dawn ritual will occupy her. She urges you to break your fast and to entertain yourself."

"Very good." As Reith ate, he asked: "Tell me, Beizi, what means that gilded skull over the door of Shosti's bedroom?"

She giggled. "That was another *Ertsu*, who was here some time ago. He fled to us to escape some trouble amongst his own folk. Noting that he had flaming hair like yours, the Protectress thought him the divine begetter of the prophecy. Let me think—he was called Bohal, or Boghel—something like unto that."

"Felix Borel?" said Reith.

"Aye, that was it. This person readily confessed to being the envoy from Heaven and labored mightily at his predestined task. For a whole revolution of Sheb, he nightly futtered our mistress, but without engendering an egg. At last, convinced that he was but an impostor, she had him beheaded in the square. The skull she had gilded as a memento, to warn any others who essayed such japes."

"A short life but a gay one," said Reith, wondering if he could still perform with his predecessor's cranium staring sightlessly at him from the shelf. "Continue, pray."

"When Tashian became Regent of Dur, the source of Shosti's error became plain. The prophecy said that the god would come in the reign of the pinchfist, but this Borel arrived ere Tashian's accession. Her Rectitude took the pinchfist to be that brigand Barré vas-Sarf. He lusts after our temple treasure and seeks to conquer us to rape us thereof. Now 'tis obvious that Gámand meant Tashian, not Barré; therefore he must have meant you and not Borel."

"Hm." Reith thought furiously. The idea of his skull's adorning the shelf beside Borel's had no appeal. "When I finish this delicious repast, may I go for a walk? I would fain explore Senarzé."

"Certes, Your Divinity. I shall summon your escort."

"Escort?"

"We cannot risk that some untimely mischance befall your mortal frame—at least, not before you have impregnated our mistress." Beizi giggled at her own insolence, opened a door, and called: "Captain Parang!"

A big, burly Krishnan in helmet and mail shirt, whom Reith recognized as the commander of the group that had brought him to Senarzé, stepped in.

"Hail, Your serene Divinity!" he said.

"Hail, mortal!" said Reith, beginning to enjoy his act. "This morning, I should like what terrans call a guided tour. Can you provide it?"

"Certes, my lord." The captain put his head out the door and whistled. A more plainly clad soldier, in a leather jacket studded with bronze buttons, came in.

"How long have you two been guarding my room?" asked Reith.

"We came on duty but a half-hour gone," said Parang, "relieving the night watch. Unlike Your Divinity, we mortals must sleep betimes."

"I will see that you get a just ration of sleep. Now let us forth."

He set out, flanked by the two soldiers. They watched him closely. Their vigilance should wear off with familiarity, he thought. Meanwhile he would learn all he could. People had escaped from more difficult places. The trick was to flee during the period when his guardians had gotten used to him but before Shosti's non-pregnancy aroused her suspicions.

142

They started with the temple. It had an ornate interior structure, bedight with columns and statues gleaming with gilt and precious stones. Reith did not pretend to judge Krishnan art. Its conventions were quite different from those of any terran art, somewhat as Mayan art differed from that of the Old World. Still, it made a fine spectacle, glittering with gold, silver, ruby, emerald, and sapphire.

"Magnificent!" said Reith, thinking flattery of local pride would do no harm.

Captain Parang and the private soldier beamed. "Our Protectress imported artists and architects from as far as Majbur and Mishé. No cost was spared to make this fane worthy of the True Faith."

At the far end of the cella, behind the altar, stood a group of statues representing Bákh, Qondyor, and Yesht, three leading divinities of the Varasto pantheon. From all Reith could gather, Shosti's cult of Ultimate Verity was a syncretic, eclectic religion, identifying the native Krishnan gods with various divinities of whom the Krishnans had heard from terran missionaries. Thus Qondyor, the Varasto war god, was supposed to correspond to Allah.

Behind the statues, occupying most of the back wall, was a mosaic, depicting a map of Zir and adjacent lands. Tesserae of gold, silver, and copper were used for settlements and boundary lines. At the center, a jeweled star represented Mount Senarzé, sending its beneficent rays (represented by silver wires) in all directions. Captain Parang explained:

"Since, according to the teachings of Ultimate Verity, everything in Heaven has its analogue upon our planet, we believe that Senarzé is the mundane equivalent of Mount Meshaq, the home of the gods. But why should I tell Your Divinity this? As a god, you already know it."

"Just where is this—" Reith began. He meant to ask

where the sectarians believed Heaven to be: on another planet, or in interstellar space, or in some other dimension.

Then he firmly shut his lips. He remembered what Pedro Arriaga, the guide originally supposed to escort Reith's tourists, once said to him; Reith had been practicing his Spanish, and Pedro said: "*En los países extrangeros, es mas prudente de no discutir la politica o la religión.*" To invite a discussion of politics or religion in this strange land might put his head on the block.

"Where is what, my lord?" said Parang.

"I did but wonder where your soldiers' quarters are."

"You shall see forthwith. Has Your Divinity finished with the temple?"

"Aye, good sir. Lead me forth."

The town of Senarzé was slummy by comparison with the magnificence of the temple. Reith followed his escorts past rows of stinking hovels to the barracks, next to the temple the largest and most substantial structure in Senarzé. Inside, it was much like any other barracks, on earth or on Krishna: plain barnlike dormitories for the single enlisted men, separate quarters for the married, and so on.

Reith kept asking Captain Parang the Ziro words for things. "Since I may be here for some time," he said, "I would fain master your local dialect."

"Dialect!" said the captain stiffening. "Divine sir, I beg you not so to denote it! Ziro is a separate language, distinct both from Durou and from Gozashtandou. It is our priceless cultural heritage, to be preserved at all costs in its logical and expressive purity."

"I crave your pardon," said Reith. "Your language, then."

"Here is the outer wall. Would Your Divinity walk

the circuit? Such a promenade is popular with the Senarzeva, especially the young who have not yet mated."

"Aye, good captain, I should like it."

As they mounted the stair to the wall, Reith mulled over the map he had seen in the temple. If he were to escape, he would need a map of his own. But how to copy that in the temple without attracting notice?

"Captain," he said at last, "when is the next service in the temple?"

"In mid-afternoon, my lord. Wherefore ask you?"

"I should like to attend. I feel the need for prayer and meditation."

"That is most edifying, my lord. But, if you will forgive my impertinence, to whom would a god like Your Divinity pray?"

The question took Reith aback, but he answered: "Why, to myself, of course. What thought you?"

"I had never considered," said Parang with a puzzled expression. "I am but a simple soldier, unqualified for theological dispute. Anyway, it shall be as you desire."

They came to the end of the wall, where the footway ended in one of the great square towers of the main gate. Reith leaned through one of the embrasures and studied the terrain. To his left, the drawbridge had been lowered again. Below the drawbridge was the ditch dug out of the saddle that joined the peak of Senarzé to the nearest mountainside.

Although Reith's experience with mountaineering had been negligible, he knew some of the principles from reading. If one had a long enough rope, one could loop the middle of the rope around a projection and rappel down, holding both strands of the rope, until one reached the bottom. Then one could let go one end of the rope and pull on the other until the whole rope came down on one.

From the ditch on down, the slope, while steep, was not entirely unscalable. There were rocky projections on which to snag the rope to lower oneself further. Lower yet, where the slope eased, there were scattered shrubs and stunted trees.

Now all he needed was a rope, a map, some food and similar supplies, and a dark night when nobody was watching him. His heart sank. While he was sure he could manage one or two of these things, he doubted that he could effect them all at once.

Days passed. By night, Fergus Reith serviced Shosti. By day, he explored every cranny of Senarzé, including the spiral stair that wound down to an underground pool. Excavated with enormous labor from solid rock, this stair provided access to water during sieges.

He inspected the great gong atop the city gate, which alerted the citizens to the approach of enemies and other emergencies. He attended services in the temple. He made a pal of Captain Parang and played games of piza to kill time. He worked at his push-ups and other calisthenics.

His attendance at the services caused some stir. Shosti insisted that he sit, not among the congregation, but up front, facing them from a gilded throne. The throne had been gathering dust in the storeroom, but the Witch of Zir commanded the temple servants to bring it out and shine it up.

Then Shosti modified the services so that the congregation addressed its prayers and flatteries directly to Reith. After a week of being called immortal, all-powerful, all-knowing, all-wise, fault-less, heroic, just, merciful, compassionate, etcetera, Reith found that once the novelty had worn off, being worshiped became a great bore. A weaker character, he thought, might make the mistake of taking all this nonsense seriously. He wondered if he would not have been wiser firmly to deny his divinity at the outset, but that was the wisdom of hindsight.

After the third day, Reith persuaded Shosti to move the throne to one side, with its back against the wall. Then he faced the altar in the middle and presented his profile to the congregation. He wanted to study the glittering temple map, which he could not do while sitting with his back to it.

The map had too many details to memorize all at once. Alone in his room, on a sheet of Krishnan paper, Reith made a rough sketch in pencil of what he could remember. During the following services, he stole glances at the map on the wall. As soon as each service was over, he went back to his rooms and corrected the errors on his map. After repeated corrections and additions, the map he drew corresponded closely enough to the original for practical purposes.

The next problem was a rope. There did not seem to be a rope walk in Senarzé. All the rope in town had been brought from elsewhere. In a seaport, there would be plenty of rope; but on this mountain top there was but little, and that already in use. Reith could not readily steal enough of this rope—say that which acted as drive belts in the windmills—with a pair of Ziro soldiers dogging his steps.

While he brooded in his room, he pulled the bell rope to summon a temple servant. Then he clapped a hand to his forehead. How stupid could he be!

The bell was answered by Gháshmi, who spoke only Zirou. Reith, however, had become adept enough at the dialect to make his wishes known. He said:

"I am curious, Gháshmi. Whither goes this rope? I know it passes through tubes to some other part of the temple, where it rings a bell."

"Will Your Divinity honor us with a visit to the servants' quarters?"

"Aye, my dear mortal, I will. Lead on."

The servants' quarters, in the cellar, were far less grand than his own. The girls were jammed into small double-deck beds, with hardly room to turn around. Gháshmi giggled.

"No male is allowed in this section, my lord," she said, "for obvious reasons. You are the first in years, but of course the rules apply not to Your Divinity." She looked at him sidelong. "If you were to command one of us to do aught that you wished, we could not gainsay you—"

Reith cleared his throat. "Later, perhaps. Right now I am more concerned with the operations of the temple."

Beside the stair leading up to the main floor was a bank of a dozen bells, bracketed to the wall. To each bell was attached the end of a pull-rope similar to that in Reith's bedchamber. The twelve ropes disappeared into holes in the ceiling. Another temple girl sat on a chair before the bells, knitting. She rose and bowed as Reith approached.

"You see, my lord," said Gháshmi, "the bells are of different sizes and hence sound different notes. One girl must ever be on duty to answer a summons. We know which part of the temple it comes from by the note. When the girl on duty goes to answer a call, she rings that little bell to one side, to warn her replacement to take her place instanter. We take the duty in rotation."

"Very interesting," said Reith peering. "Which bell summons you to my chambers?"

"This one," said Gháshmi. "Your Divinity honors us with your interest."

She and the other girl chattered at him, giving him details of temple routine. He finally begged off, saying he had to wash up for the next service.

• • •

The next time Reith prowled the city, he came upon a house whose owner was tarring his roof. Feigning interest, he persuaded the Krishnan to come down his ladder and explain.

"You see, Your serene Divinity," said the Krishnan, "I put the cold pitch in this barrel and light the little fire underneath. When the pitch is melted, I scoop up a bucketful, carry it up to the roof, and apply it with this brush."

All this was obvious. Nevertheless, Reith kept the fellow talking. Then the house owner looked into his bucket and said: "Oh, my lord, my pitch has cooled and solidified! Now must I dump it back in the barrel to melt it again."

"My apologies; I am sorry," said Reith.

"A god need never apologize, Your Divinity!"

"I do so natheless. A god should not be careless with his worshipers' goods. May I see that cold pitch?"

"Certes, Your Divinity. Here."

Reith dug his fingers into the pitch and scooped out a lump the size of a golf ball. The pitch was still hot enough to scorch his fingers. Wincing, he held on.

"May I keep this, to remind me of my divine duty?" he asked.

"Your Divinity is more than welcome. You honor me by your request. Would you like the whole bucketful?"

"Nay, goodman; this will suffice. Good day."

Followed by his escorts, Reith walked back to the temple, tossing the lump of pitch from hand to hand. One of the soldiers, the stout, heavy-set Lieutenant Khonj, asked:

"Permit me to ask Your Divinity what your godlike purpose was, in begging that lump of pitch?"

"Just an experiment I had in mind," said Reith carelessly. "Know you not that I am a god of inventors among others? I had an idea for a new device."

"But my lord, you could have asked one of us to fetch you all the pitch you could use!"

"The idea came to me but now. I wished to strike whilst the iron was hot, as we say in Heaven. But I appreciate your assiduity."

That night, Captain Parang had the evening shift. When Beizi asked Reith if he was ready to join Shosti, Reith said:

"Kindly tell Her Rectitude I am fatigued. I need a night out with the boys, as we put it in Heaven. I shall join her after she is asleep; I perform better in the morning anyway."

"I will tell my lady."

"And ask Captain Parang to step in, will you?"

When the officer appeared, Reith said: "How about another game of piza, old fellow?"

"Your Divinity is too kind."

"And no pretending to make mistakes so that I shall win! I your god am a sporting god." Reith got out the board and the pieces. "I'll tell you what. Every time one of us loses a piece, he shall take a drink."

"How much of a drink, my lord?"

"This much." Reith produced a large jug of kvad and two small silver tumblers. "One of these full. They are supposed to have come down from Gámand the Unshorn, but I believe it not. Gámand was an ascetic who never touched strong drink or owned costly baubles. I stole these from the display cabinet in the temple."

"My lord!" Parang sounded shocked. "Whatever a god does is good by definition. So how can you speak of yourself as 'stealing' aught? The temple and all in it is yours. If a mortal accused Your Divinity of theft, 'twere blasphemy."

"Well, what's the use of being a god if one cannot take one's own name in vain? Black or white?"

150

The game began. Soon Reith lost a piece and swallowed his kvad at a gulp. Moving more cautiously, he presently captured one of Parang's men; then another.

So it went. For several days, Reith had been studying the game, playing with anyone he could find; the temple servants, the soldiers, even Shosti. Hence he soon outclassed Parang, who was forced to drink two or three tumblers of kvad to Reith's one.

When they were halfway through the fourth game, Captain Parang was visibly affected. He yawned, mumbled, and made patent efforts to stay awake and alert.

Reith saw a chance for a rare move, capturing three of Parang's men at once. He made the move, swept up the pieces, and said:

"Now you must drink a triple, my friend. . . ."

A gentle wheeze, the Krishnan version of a snore, answered him.

Reith glanced at the time candle on the dresser. All was quiet. He picked up the jug of kvad and tiptoed to the door.

Outside, Parang's back-up was sitting against the wall. At sight of Reith, he rubbed his eyes and scrambled up. Reith murmured:

"Good Private Ghirch, we are having a hot game within and would not be disturbed. Would a swig of this ease your watch?"

The Krishnan's eyes lit up. "Aye verily, Your Divinity!"

Reith left the jug with the soldier, returned to his room, and snuffed out all but one of the candles. He took the lump of pitch from under his pillow and warmed it over the remaining candle until it was plastic.

Then he went swiftly through the passage to the servants' quarters. At the foot of the long stair, he

151

found one of the girls sitting in the chair before the bank of bells, trying, in the feeble light, to read a Krishnan book. The book consisted of a long strip of native paper folded zigzag, with a pair of wooden covers.

"Hail, good Jazeri!" he said as the girl rose and bowed. "Would you do your god a small favor?"

"Aught you say, my lord."

"Well then, how about a cup of hot *chaven*?" This was a non-alcoholic, mildly stimulating Krishnan drink. "I have drunk so much kvad, gaming with Captain Parang, that my mortal body needs a sobering draft."

"At once, Your Divinity!" Jazeri scuttled away.

Reith examined the bells. Into the one whose rope extended to his bedchamber, he inserted the lump of warm pitch. He pressed it between the bell and the clapper, pushing the clapper into the yielding surface with his thumbs. Now the clapper was firmly stuck to the bell and would not ring.

Then he took out his pocket knife and sawed the rope, where it came down behind the bell. He cut through all but the last few fibers, so that any vigorous pull would break the rope.

He put the knife away as he heard Jazeri's returning footsteps. He leisurely sipped the chaven, flattering Jazeri and her fellow temple workers. He praised the cleanliness of the temple and the high polish on the decorations. The girl purred.

When he had downed the cup, he handed it to Jazeri and mounted the stairs. Back in Reith's bedchamber, Parang still slept. A peek out the door showed that Private Ghirch had likewise fallen asleep.

Reith stepped to the bell pull and gave a vigorous tug. A meter of rope snaked out of the hole in the wall and was not withdrawn. Reith kept pulling until the entire length tumbled down before him.

He wound the rope around his waist, under the cloth-of-gold tunic. Then he looked at Parang. The captain was dead to the world. His hooded cloak lay on the floor by the door.

Reith wondered if he could unbuckle the captain's baldric and get his sword. Fearing that this would arouse Parang, he decided instead to unhook the captain's scabbard from the baldric. Captain Parang wheezed on.

Lacking a proper sword belt, Reith stuck the scabbard through his emerald-studded girdle. The arrangement was uncomfortable but would have to do.

From under his bed, Reith recovered the sack of biscuits he had secreted. Since he had begun collecting them days earlier, some must be pretty stale; but that was no matter. He got the map from his desk.

He donned Parang's cloak, pulling the hood well down. He was tempted to write a note saying that Captain Parang was not to be blamed for his escape, since Reith had tricked him. He liked the old Krishnan; but, with his meager knowledge of Krishnan writing, it would take him an hour to compose an intelligible note. While he hoped that nothing would happen to Parang, Reith put his own life and those of his tourists first.

Soon after, Reith mounted the stone stair to the top of the city wall, near the main gate. A sentry saw him, saluted at the sight of an officer's cloak, and continued his rounds. The sentries in front of the temple had done likewise.

With sweaty hands and pounding heart, Reith unwound the pull rope from his waist. He slipped the bight in the middle over the merlon next to the gate tower, scrambled through the embrasure, got his scabbard caught crosswise in the opening, worked it loose, and lowered himself down the outer face of the wall.

As he did so, a horrid thought struck him. In preparing for his flight, he had tried to think of everything; but, in his nervous haste, he had forgotten to change his shoes. He still wore the thin, ornate, gilded footwear, scarcely more than bedroom slippers, that formed a part of his temple costume. He had meant to don the stout boots in which he had been captured and which he used in his walks about the city. These, however, still stood peacefully in his clothes closet, and it was too late to go back for them.

X.

A PAIR OF BOOTS

By feeling around in the dark, moving slowly lest he tumble down the slope, Fergus Reith found, near the base of the wall, an outcropping of rock. He looped his bight of the rope around the projection and backed down the slope, a step at a time.

The night was overcast. This helped to hide Reith from Krishnan eyes, since Krishnan nights whence all three moons were absent at once occurred not often. On the other hand, he could just barely make out the forms of the hillside. The slope near the top was almost vertical. If he slipped, he would go bouncing down base-over-apex.

Then he felt more solid footing beneath his feet. Straining his eyes, he saw he had reached a narrow ledge. Below, the slope eased.

Reith halted and began to pull on one end of the rope. The rope came down, while the other end disappeared into the darkness above. Then something caught.

Reith jerked the rope, which remained snagged. With both hands, he gave his strongest tug, almost losing his balance.

Reith recovered, but sounds from above indicated that his final jerk had loosened the rock around which he had looped the rope. The sound swiftly waxed and changed to a series of thumps as the stone, gathering speed, began to bounce. Reith knew that a boulder, weighing perhaps thirty to sixty kilos, was headed towards him.

The ledge was not spacious enough for dodging, even if he had time and could have seen the stone's approach. He flattened himself against the slope like a lizard, pressing himself into the rock and dirt as tightly as he could.

The boulder struck above his head, bounced, and cleared him by a few centimeters. He felt the wind of its passage on his neck. Trembling with relief, he heard diminishing thumps as the boulder bounded on down the slope. Several smaller stones followed. One struck his shoulder with bruising force, but he paid it no heed.

When he stopped shaking, he peered into the darkness below. The slope seemed gentle enough so that, backing down and using his hands, he could make the rest of the descent without rappeling. He gathered up his rope and resumed his descent.

Reith was nearing the base of the crag, where the slope was gentle enough to walk facing forward, when a deep bell-note sounded above. It was the great gong over the main gate. Lights bobbed and flickered along the city wall far above, like a swarm of agitated fireflies. A rattle of chains indicated that the draw-bridge was being lowered.

As fast as he dared, Reith picked his way over the talus at the foot of the peak of Senarzé and pushed into the scrubby forest at the bottom. He tripped over stones and fallen logs and blundered into the little stream that trickled down the vale. He kept on forcing his way through the growth.

At sunrise, Reith wearily sat on a log and pulled out his map. His gaudy clothes were dirty and torn; he was bruised, scratched, and bug-bitten. Even at the snail's pace at which he had had to move, he must have gone at least half a dozen kilometers. Senarzé was no longer in sight.

Staring about, he thought that, if he climbed a ridge to the east and went down the other side, he could reach a stream that took him close to Mount Kehar. Once he had sighted that snow cap, he could, if his strength held out, reach Gha'id and the railroad camp.

Fatigue, however, was catching up with him. He would have to eat and find some hidden place to sleep. His feet hurt from walking over sticks and stones in his fragile, disintegrating temple shoes.

He was munching a stale biscuit and washing it down with cold water from the stream when a sound made him start. A game trail ran up the hillside, and down this trail appeared an armed Krishnan.

Reith and the warrior sighted each other at the same instant. Reith recognized Lieutenant Khonj, who had been one of his regular escorts. At the sight of Reith, Khonj shouted:

"*Ohé!* Here he is!"

He advanced upon Reith, sweeping out his sword and hitching a buckler around to grasp in his left hand. Most Krishnans were right-handed.

Reith jumped up and drew, his exhaustion forgotten. "What would you?"

"Your head, my fine impostor!" said Khonj. "Order of the Protectress."

The Krishnan rushed upon Reith. Khonj came

forward with his left foot advanced and the buckler out
before him. His right arm was raised, with his fist
above his right ear, so that his sword was horizontal
with the hilt towards Reith and the point projecting
backwards.

Evidently Khonj relied on his edge. From that
stance, he could slash at Reith without having to raise
his blade first, and he could easily parry a downright
cut at his head.

Reith took the position that Heggstad had taught
him, right foot advanced and sword held in front of
him, point towards his antagonist and slightly above
the horizontal. Although he had learned the rudiments
of saber technique at Novorecife, Heggstad's teachings
had not shown him how to face a man with a shield.
There had not been time.

Khonj launched a downright cut. It came with a
stunning force, but Reith got his blade up in time to
parry. The swords clanged, and the force of the blow
almost knocked the weapon from Reith's hand. A
backhand cut he evaded by scrambling backward.

"Stand and die, coward!" shouted Khonj. "*Ohé!* To
me! I have the blasphemer!"

There was no reply. Reith guessed that Khonj had
become separated from his search party.

"There's no point in fighting me," said Reith. "Let's
talk this over."

"Ha!" said Khonj. "A vile earthman cozens us into
worshiping him as a god! No reasons, eh?"

"Not my idea," said Reith. "You people insisted I
was a god, and I didn't feel I could dispute the matter."

He parried another slash and riposted with a thrust
over Khonj's shield. Khonj brought his shield up to
block the thrust, but Reith's point still ripped the
Krishnan's tunic and scratched his shoulder. Khonj
gave back a step. He paused as if uncertain how to
handle the earthman.

Then he came on again with a flurry of slashes. His blade was a little shorter than Reith's but heavier. This made his cuts hard to stop but also slowed them enough so that Reith could parry them. When Khonj hesitated between cuts, Reith lunged at the Krishnan's face. The lunge went awry, missing the Krishnan's head; but Khonj threw up his shield and gave back a step, panting.

"You're being foolish," said Reith. "I mean Senarzé no harm."

"Liar! You caused the death of my beloved friend, Captain Parang."

"I'm sorry. I liked him."

"A fine way to show it! Now your head shall decorate the city gate beside his."

"I had to escape. You know what befell my predecessor, Borel."

"You should have told us at the outset you were but mortal."

"Belike; but I knew not what—"

Reith broke off as Khonj attacked again, raining blows. Back and forth they went, stumbling over the uneven ground. Reith made cuts and lunges, but Khonj stopped them with his shield, and his whistling slashes kept Reith dodging, parrying, and backing.

Sweat soaked through Reith's cloth-of-gold tunic and ran down Khonj's dust-caked face from under his spired helmet. Between times they stood, panting and glaring.

Evidently Khonj was determined to kill Reith, no matter what. Reith gave up the argument, saving his breath for fighting. The next time Khonj came on, Reith feinted a stop thrust at Khonj's face.

At that instant, a stone turned under Khonj's foot, causing him a small stumble. Hence, in bringing up his buckler to block Reith's thrust, he jerked the shield much higher than was needed. Reith lunged quickly at

Khonj's left leg, where it emerged from beneath his tunic. He felt his point bite meat. Before he could recover, the heavy blade came whizzing down on his head.

Reith thought he was dead. Although the blow staggered him, the blade was stopped by the folds of the turban; the edge bit deeply enough to cause him only a slight scalp wound. As Reith reeled back, Khonj stepped forward to follow him. Then Khonj's wounded leg buckled beneath him, and Khonj sprawled amid the stones.

Obeying his terran habits, Reith lowered his sword and stepped forward, saying: "I'm sorry. Can I help—"

Teeth bared, Khonj propped himself up on one elbow and swung his sword at Reith's legs. Reith saved his feet by leaping backward.

"Son of a bitch!" said Reith; then in Zirou: "You truly list to slay me, do you not?"

"Your head or mine!" snarled Khonj. The Krishnan got to all fours and began to crawl towards Reith, sword in hand.

"*Baghan!*" said Reith, wishing he knew more expletives. He picked up a five-kilo stone and hurled it at Khonj's head. The missile clanged off the Krishnan's helmet, bowling Khonj over. Khonj clapped his hands to his head, dropping his sword. Reith sprang forward and kicked the sword out of reach. Then he went over and picked it up.

Khonj sat up, still holding his head. A trickle of blue-green blood ran down the side of his face, where the stone had dented his helmet. The hose on his left leg was already soaked with the same fluid.

"Well, slay me and have done!" said Khonj.

"Why?" said Reith. "I eat not Krishnans. I need not your hide for leather, and your head were too heavy to carry off as a trophy. So what use could I make of your carcass?"

"What would you, then?"

"I want your boots."

"Take them off my corpse, if you dare!"

"If you insist." Reith picked up another stone and made a baseball windup.

"You would pound me to death in that unsoldierly manner?" said Khonj.

"Why not? You'd be equally dead in any case."

"A peasantly way of fighting, unworthy of a warrior."

"As you please." Reith threw the stone, which thumped against Khonj's chest and bounced off.

Khonj groaned but grabbed the stone as it rolled away. He tried to throw it at Reith, but his throw went wild.

"You know not our terran games," said Reith, picking up another stone.

"Wait," said Khonj.

"Well?"

"You leave me no choice. I was a fool to fight an *Ertsu*; they scorn our notions of honor and chivalry. Take the boots. I shall probably bleed to death ere I regain Senarzé, but no matter."

"Pull them off for me," said Reith, nervous about placing himself within reach of Khonj's powerful hands.

After a struggle, Khonj got the right boot off. He tried to remove the left but failed because of the pain in his wounded leg.

"Lie back," said Reith.

Holding his sword poised, he gingerly approached Khonj's supine form. With his left hand he grasped the heel of the boot and tugged, watching Khonj's face against a sudden move.

Khonj lay back, gripping a couple of rocks, and groaned. His face turned pale under its greenish complexion. At last Reith got the boot off and retreated to a safe distance.

"You must have the biggest feet on Krishna, my friend," he said as he examined the boots.

"Mock me not," muttered Khonj.

Reith experimented with the boots. He finally took off and unwound his turban, now soaked with blood from his scalp cut. By cutting the long strip of cloth in half and winding each half around a foot, he could make do with the boots. He rose and gathered up his provisions, saying:

"Farewell, Lieutenant. Since I have no use for two swords, I shall stick yours in yonder tree, where you can recover it. I shall also leave you these temple shoes; they are falling apart but may be better than nought.

"If you want my advice, it were to desert. You know what Shosti does to servants who fail to carry out her commands. You see, I really have nought against you."

"Of course you have nought!" grunted Khonj. "To you off-worlders, we are but interesting animals. You have no more sentiment for us as thinking, feeling beings than we have for a strange unha or kargán. To you we are mere things."

"Please yourself," said Reith, turning away. "Some of my best friends are Krishnans."

"Think not to escape!" Khonj called after him. "The Koloftuma will surely track you down."

Reith sheathed his notched blade and took the game trail down which Khonj had come. As the shrubbery closed in, he heard a final shout—doubtless a parting defiance or insult—from Khonj. He headed up the ridge towards the valley, which, he believed, would bring him within sight of Mount Kehar.

Sigvard Lund looked up from checking a sight with his archaic surveying instrument and exclaimed: "*För Guds skull!* Are you not that tour-guide leader?"

Reith mumbled a reply as he limped out of the

woods, using his scabbarded sword as a walking stick. His temple finery was in rags. Such of his face as was not masked by a coppery stubble was caked with dirt; a dark-brown stripe of dried blood ran down his forehead from his scalp wound. Whereas he had been lean before, now he was skeletally gaunt and hollow-eyed. He staggered toward Lund, who rushed to support him and shouted:

"Kenneth! Where are you?"

"Here," said Strachan, stepping out from behind a pile of railroad ties. "Loshtie!" he cried. "If it isna ma brither Scot, aul' Fergus! We thocht ye deed!"

"I'm alive, all right," said Reith, "but just barely. Can you guys get me down to the camp? I don't know if I could walk it."

Lund shouted to the nearest Krishnan: "Fetch the nearest bishtar! Ken, you take him down, be so good."

When Reith had been boosted into the howdah and joined by Strachan, the latter said: "What do you need most, Fergus? Any bones broken or aucht?"

"The first thing," said Reith, "is your first-aid kit. I've got some broken blisters that may be infected."

"I'll fix them, but dinna worry. Very few Krishnan microörganisms can live in a terran host."

"That's hopeful, anyway. The next thing is a bucket full of hot water to soak my feet in. Ever try to wear a pair of Krishnan boots three sizes too large over thirty kilometers of forested mountains, with rain every other day? And the next thing is a good meal. I finished my last biscuit three days ago, and I could eat this bishtar, hide, hair, and all. But tell me, what's become of my tourists? Has Barré still got them?"

"Aye, he has. His man and Tashian's still meet to chaffer, but they get nowhere. They're as suspicious of each other as Qarar and the Witch of the Va'andao."

"Has Barré sent out any of my people's ears or heads to speed things up?"

"No; at least, not yet. I hear he's waiting for a lucky day before doing aucht so drastic."

"Then I've got to get back to Baianch, pronto. Can you arrange it?"

"Man, you're in no shape to travel! You need rest and loving care."

"Never mind what shape I'm in. I've tried everything I can think of to spring my geese, and nothing works. I've got to see if Mjipa can help."

"If Percy can't, nobody can," said Strachan. "But tell me where you've been! Barré sent word you'd escaped and supposed you'd come back to us. He demanded you back, on pain of killing one or more of your tourists. We told him we hadn't seen you, but he didn't believe us. Where were you all that time?"

Reith gave a résumé of his experiences with the Witch of Zir. "Where's Mrs. Whitney Scott? She was left behind in Gha'id."

"I took her back to Baianch on the train. Tashian's put her up in his palace."

"What happened to that Lieutenant Gandubán, who got away when Barré caught us? Did he make good his escape?"

"Aye; but, when Tashian found out, he cashiered the fellow from the army. Just like the Regent, not to give his officer enough men to do his job and then to sack him when the job's not done. Gandubán's lucky to have kept his head. But look here, laddie, you must stay with us long enough to get some strength back. We can't have you dying on the way to Baianch."

They argued amiably until Reith agreed to remain at the camp at least one day before setting forth again. Two days later, washed, shaved, clad in the spare clothing he had left at the camp, and filled out after a series of enormous meals, he boarded a small rail car drawn by a single aya. The vehicle was an ordinary Krishnan carriage, corresponding to a terran barouche

164

and adapted to rail use by flanged wheels. Strachan rode with Reith, while a Krishnan driver up front kept the animal moving.

Strachan explained that he and Lund used the vehicle for inspection trips. It was twice as fast as a bishtar-drawn train, so that they made the three-day journey to Baianch in two days. When, after leaving Jizorg, they met the daily head-on on the single track, they pried the carriage off the rails and pulled it to one side to let the train pass.

As they clattered into the Baianch terminal after dark on the second day, Reith said: "That's better time than you could make with a horse on earth. We must have gone three or four hundred kilometers. That's how many hoda?"

"Six legs have advantages," said Strachan.

"How can I find Percy Mjipa?"

"I'd start with the chief of police, but almost any upper bureaucrat in the Old Palace could tell you. Before you do that, you ought to pay your respects to the Regent."

"But I'm in a hurry, Ken! With my tourists in danger, I can't fool around with all that damned ceremony."

"Tashian'll be affronted if you don't. This isn't the earth, you know. More haste, less speed. You'll get further if you follow routine. These folk don't have our sense of time."

At length, Strachan persuaded Reith to abide by protocol. He clapped Reith on the back, saying:

"Guid nicht, laddie! You know what I come to town for. Care to come along and dip your wick?"

"Thanks, but I had enough of that with Shosti to last me quite a while."

The morning after his arrival, Reith stood in the small chamber of private audience. He faced Tashian bag-Gárin, clad in his usually shabby black; a couple of Regent's officials, and the inevitable guards. For over a Krishnan hour, they grilled Reith about Barré vas-Sarf and his army, and about Senarzé and its Protectress. One official said to the regent:

"Your Excellency, methinks a modest subsidy to Dame Shosti might so strengthen her in Barré's rear that he durst not interfere with us."

"What had you in mind?" said Tashian.

"Oh, an initial sportula of ten thousand—"

The Regent uttered a strangled sound. "Are you mad, to start with so lavish an offer? She'd scent wealth to be had for the taking and demand thrice the amount. Nay rather, let's begin with a mere thousand...."

The argument rattled on. Reith waited until both disputants paused for breath and said: "Your Excellence, may I withdraw? I fain would find my fellow earthman Mjipa."

"Aye, you may go, Master Reese. You'll find your man at the new consulate building, just completing, on Bourujird Avenue near the Sea Gate. Oh, wait an instant. Come back ere eventide for a supper with Douri and me. You shall tell us more of your adventures."

"I thank Your Excellency," said Reith, bowing his way out.

Near the waterfront, he found the towering black diplomat overseeing the final touches on a new but modest two-story house. In fluent Durou, Mjipa was berating a Duro plasterer for doing a sloppy job around the front door frame. He swung around as Reith approached.

"What ho, Mr. Reith!" he said, wringing Reith's hand. "There was a rumor that you'd returned from the dead. I didn't believe it—you know these natives—but I'm jolly glad to see it wasn't exaggerated. What of your trippers?"

"That what I'm here to see about."

"Hm. I see we shall need a talk. Hang it all, I hate to leave these beggars unsupervised—turn your back five minutes and they've done something wrong—but duty calls. Come to my digs."

Mjipa occupied a small apartment three blocks from the consulate. Here Reith met Mjipa's wife, a black woman taller than Reith (who was above average) and massive. She must, Reith thought, outweigh him two to one.

"Mr. Reith," she said, "I'm glad to see somebody can make Percy take time off. He's what you call a workaholic; thinks he has to watch every little detail."

"You try getting Krishnans to do anything without watching every little detail," said Mjipa, "and you'll bloody well see what happens. Pour us a drink, will you, my dear?"

"Will you and Mrs. Mjipa be moving into the new building?" asked Reith.

"For a little while. Once I have the consulate running, Ishimoto's slated to take over. He's a sound enough man but routine-minded. Then I'm to have a crack at setting up another one in Zanid, the capital of Balhib. They've got some weird customs out there, even by Krishnan standards, so it ought to present a challenge. But, how about your tourists?"

Reith again told his story. Mjipa listened, chin in hand.

"I wonder," he said at last. "I haven't any force to use on Barré, and he jolly well knows it. If the World Federation weren't a lot of squeamish old ladies, saying we dare not protect our own against outrages for fear of looking like bloody imperialists.... But never mind that."

"Could we offer a cash ransom?" said Reith.

"Barré's already sent word he's not interested. Of course, that may be a bluff. Even if it were, Novo wouldn't consider paying for fear of setting a precedent. Tashian's too stingy, and I have no private fortune to dip into. Besides, I don't want to encourage the blighters, any more than Novo does. Too bad your female witch doctor isn't the real thing, so she could put a spell on Barré."

"I'm thinking. Just a minute," said Reith. He closed his eyes, searching his memory. "Barré said something about wanting a new religion to consolidate his political position. If we could offer him one...."

"Maybe he does, but he wants guns even more."

"I'm still thinking." Reith stared at Mjipa. "Do you know an Indian missionary, Ganesh Kosambi?"

"An Indian Indian or a Red Indian?"

"An East Indian. One of the Lords of Light people."

"Seems to me I've heard of him, but I've never met him."

"Have you ever attended one of their services?"

"No," said Mjipa.

"Well, I have. I was thinking: With a turban and one of those orange robes, you'd make a pretty good Indian yourself."

"Oh, rubbish, my dear fellow! Anybody can see I'm of the Negroid race. My frizzy hair would give me away instantly. Makes a damned good natural sun helmet in the tropics, though."

"But your hair couldn't be seen under the turban; anyway, what do Krishnans know of terran ethnology?"

"Look, old boy, are you proposing to pass me off as some bloody cultist missionary?"

"Yes, sir. Now wait!" said Reith as Mjipa opened his mouth to protest. "Barré himself told me he was inclined toward the Lords of Light cult, and you haven't heard my idea...."

After an hour of argument, Mjipa said: "Well, damn it, I suppose I've got to try out this mad scheme of yours, since nothing else seems to work. Can't let the side down. The things I'm called on to do on my rotten pay. . . . At least, if I survive, I can use it to demand a step up on the civil service list."

Reith sat at a table with the Regent and the Douri. A servitor stood behind each of the diners. The candle flames were reflected on the silvered breastplates of the guards who stood in the doorway.

". . . . and so I found myself installed in the Temple of Ultimate Verity," said Reith. "I must say it was luxurious enough."

"What wanted the Protectress with you?" asked Vázni.

Reith made a vague motion. "Some silly idea they have, about a red-haired savior from the stars."

"Was that all?" asked Tashian, looking sharply at Reith.

"Well—ah—I really know not the details of their theology. . . ."

Tashian smiled. "Master Reese, I am better informed than you give me credit for. 'Tis Dame Shosti's whimwham that an earthman like unto you will beget upon her a world-saving hero. I have my sources, you see."

"And did you in sooth futter the Witch?" asked Vázni eagerly. "Do the dames of our world give as keen a pleasure as those of yours? Why, Master Reese, wherefore glows your face so red? Are you ill? Is the heat excessive?"

Reith cleared his throat. "Let's say I did what I had to do to save my skin. Earthmen of my sort discuss not such matters so freely."

Tashian raised his antennae. "Indeed? You must belong to a tribe or sect other than that of your fellow *Ertsu*, Master Strachan. He has no such reserves, boasting rather of his lubricity. Of course, as you doubtless know, customs differ widely among the nations of this world. Some regulate the sexual act most stringently, while others let men and women couple as they list. Left you the harridan with egg?"

Reith shook his head. "That were impossible, sir. Earthmen and Krishnans are as mutually sterile as—as an aya and a shomal. Professor Mulroy, among my tourists, could explain it; something to do with the tiny cells whence living things originate. The—the—our word is *chromosomes*—fit not together."

"I can see how that might be," said Tashian, looking at Reith from under lowered antennae. "'Tis a subject of hot dispute amongst our learned ones. Forsooth, I've heard rumors of such an hybrid but have never seen one, albeit I've told my agents to search the land for such."

"Your Excellency may take it for granted that such rumors are baseless. I'm no scientist, but I studied such things when I was a teacher."

"So, if one of you beings wedded a wench from our ruling families, in hopes of founding a dynasty, I ween he'd be disappointed?"

"Certeš, Your Excellency."

Vázni broke in. "Since you'll tell us nought of your prowess in the Witch's bed, then let us hear of your escape from her embraces!"

When Reith had finished his narrative, she said: "By the green eyes of Hoi, Master Reese, you may not be a god. But, if half of what you tell be sooth, you are a true hero. You deserve a reward."

"Oh, I did nought really—" Reith began.

Vázni, however, got up and came around the table. She sat down on Reith's lap and kissed him with fierce intentness.

"There!" she said. "Did I it rightly? This terran custom has but lately spread to our barbarous northland."

Reith drew a deep breath. Across the table, Tashian beamed complacently.

"Th-thank you, Douri," said Reith.

"And now," said Tashian, "what are your plans?"

"I leave for Gha'id on the morrow with Mjipa, for one more attempt to free my folk."

"May the luck of Maibud the Light-Fingered go with you," said the Regent. "When you return, we shall have further matters to discuss. There are many possibilities."

"Your Excellence means, if I return," said Reith.

Vázni spoke: "A veritable Qarar like you cannot fail; the stars in their courses fight for you. When you come back, if my cousin prove as niggardly as is his wont, I'll see to your reward myself."

XI.

TRUMPET AND DRUM

Fergus Reith and Percy Mjipa sat with Strachan and Lund in the engineers' sitting room at the railroad camp. They glumly stared at a six-foot strip of crimson cloth, festooned around Mjipa's neck. Mjipa said:

"Every time I make a sudden move, the damned thing comes unstuck. When I joined the consular service, nobody told me I should have to know how to wind a turban. Bloody stupid native costumery!"

"The thing to do," said Reith, "is to wind it up and have someone stitch it together."

"Not quite sporting, I suppose," said Mjipa, "but our bandit king won't know the difference. Who's got a needle and thread?"

"I know a good seamstress in Gha'id," said Strachan. "Khar's wife Gulási."

"Can you fetch her?" said Lund.

"Aye."

173

"Well, try not to be murdered by her kin, be so good."

"I've done her nae damage!" said Strachan. "Merely a bit of harmless fun while her mate was off fishing."

"I know, but these villagers have some quaint ideas on sex. Now, Mr. Mjipa, what shall be your Indian name? Barré might have heard of you, so you can't use your own. Besides, an obviously Bantu name might arouse suspicion."

"Well," said Mjipa, "who's that chap you were telling me about, Fergus? The one who runs the Lords of Light in Majbur?"

"Ganesh Kosambi," said Reith. "You can't use his name, because Barré might have heard of him, too. Anyway, you're not at all like him; he's short and fat. Same objections apply to Judge Keshavachandra."

"Let me think, then," said Mjipa. "There's a consul on Vishnu from India, Vasant Panikkar. I'm sure he's never set foot on Krishna outside of Novo, so I'll jolly well borrow his name."

Several days later, Reith and Mjipa, the latter in saffron robe and crimson turban, mounted two bishtars. The baggage of each was handed up. Reith's baggage consisted of a heavy canvas sack, which jingled.

The railroad base camp had changed since the abduction. Tashian had sent a company of soldiers, who had fortified the camp with a ditch and a log stockade. Under a gruff captain, the soldiers drilled smartly, making camp noisy with shouted commands and the clatter of practice weapons.

The soldiers opened the massive timber gate to let the bishtars out. The animals plodded up the switchback road to the construction site. There, they were told, Barré's envoy awaited them.

At the site, Reith climbed down one of the rope

ladders hanging from the howdah. He shook hands with Barré's man, an elderly Ziro named Ramost, saying:

"You must excuse the Reverend Vasant Panikkar from shaking hands. He fears damage to his aura."

"Ah," said Ramost. "I see. But tell me, Master Reese, wherefore sit you two earthmen upon two bishtars, when one such beast can bear six or eight riders with ease?"

"His Reverence is too sacred to share his mount," said Reith. "The radiations of his holiness might harm a mere mortal placed too close to him."

"Ah, I see. Are you ready, forth to sally?"

"Aye, sir."

Reith climbed back into his howdah, while Ramost mounted an aya and trotted off into the forest. The bishtars lumbered after.

For the rest of the day, Reith and Mjipa were bounced around their howdahs as their mounts plodded up and down sloping trails, splashed through mountain streams, and pushed through dense vegetation where the trail had become overgrown. Branches bearing many-colored leaves whipped the faces of the riders, who fended them off. After Mjipa had twice lost his turban, he took it off and put it on the floor of his howdah.

The day was hot and humid, so that Reith's clothes were soon sweat-soaked. Once they crossed a swamp, where the bishtars' legs sank in until the water was up to the animals' bellies. Reith had visions of being mired for good. The bishtars' feet, however, came readily out of their holes with sucking sounds.

Towards evening, a sharp challenge sounded. Ramost answered. A pair of armed Ziruma wheeled out of the forest on ayas and escorted the visitors to Barré's camp. Mjipa put on his crimson turban.

It occurred to Reith that this camp differed from the

other. Barré must have moved his base to forestall a surprise by the forces of Dur. As Reith descended, Barré stepped forward and shook hands, saying:

"I should never have believed it, Master Reese! Little did I think that, once free of my trammels, you'd wittingly put yourself back in my power. You must be that which I thought existed not amongst the *Ertsuma:* a true idealist—or else the biggest fool on either of our worlds. What brings you hither?"

"I've brought you your Lords of Light missionary," said Reith, "hoping thus perhaps to soften your demands upon my people."

"Well, well. Think not that I'll let them go for that reason; their ransom remains as before. Still, as a man of honor, I shall take into account the favor you've done me. You, sir, may leave my camp as you list."

"I thank Your Altitude," said Reith. "And now let me present the Reverend Vasant Panikkar...."

Reith was explaining why the Reverend could not shake hands when a feminine shriek, of terran timbre, told that his tourists had learned of his return. They rushed upon him, brushing Barré aside. The women kissed him and the men wrung his hands and pounded his back. Under cover of the noise, he said to Aimé Jussac:

"We're going to try something. When the Reverend says 'Go!', you must all jump up, run to the bishtars, and climb into the howdahs. Quietly; not a peep out of anyone! Pass the word along."

Silvester Pride was looking closely at Mjipa, who stood statuesquely with his hands clasped behind his back. Pride's raucous voice rose: "Say, aren't you that guy we met—"

"This," said Reith loudly, "is His Holiness, the Reverend Vasant Panikkar, a bishop of the Church of the Lords of Light. Don't talk to him, Silvester. He

needs to meditate and send out vibrations of goodness."

"What the hell you talking about, Fearless?" said
Pride. "You said you never believed these con men—"

Guzmán-Vidal snarled into Pride's ear: "Shut up,
idiota, or I twist your balls off with my bare hands!"

Grumbling, Pride subsided. "Thanks, Santiago,"
said Reith.

Barré asked: "When, good my sirs, will His
Reverence have his first service? I'm fain to see how
my brave men take it."

Receiving a nod from Mjipa, Reith replied: "Roqir's
disk nears the horizon. If you'll suffer us to clean
ourselves and rest a little space, His Reverence would
conduct prayers at sunset."

"So be it," said Barré.

In the tent assigned to Reith and Mjipa, Reith
clapped a hand to his forehead. "Oh, God, what a
stupid ass I am! No matter how quiet our people try to
be, they'll make enough noise to arouse the Ziruma.
Why didn't I bring some noise-making gadget to
drown them out?"

"I should have thought of it likewise," said Mjipa.
"But perhaps all is not lost. Do Barré's men use drums
or trumpets?"

"Both. They beat a drum for close-order drills and
blow a trumpet for signals. Maybe we can borrow a
drum."

"Both would be useful."

"But we'd have to get one of the Ziruma to blow the
trumpet, and he couldn't do that while lying on his
face."

"Could you or any of your tourists play the thing?"

"I've never blown a horn in my life. As for the
others, even if one could, he couldn't blow and run for
the bishtars at the same time."

L. Sprague de Camp

"Too bad we don't have Strachan with his bagpipes. Look, old boy, you borrow the drum and the trumpet while I go over my notes. When the time comes, you can beat the drum while I play the trumpet."

"Can you play a trumpet?"

"I could toot a jolly good bugle when I was a Botswana Boy Scout. That was many years ago, but I'll have a go at this native instrument anyway."

Reith went out, found Barré, and explained that the service called for sacred music. He returned to find Mjipa, wearing spectacles with the bows poked up under his turban, poring over his notes.

"Here you are," said Reith.

"Smashing!" said Mjipa. "Let's have a look at this thing."

He raised the gleaming brass horn. A discordant squall came from the trumpet.

"Sounds like a dying dinosaur," said Reith.

"Takes practice, that's all." Mjipa essayed a few more toots and found the scale. He played a few bars of a tune.

"Let's hope we don't have any connoisseurs of terran music among the Ziruma," said Reith.

"If you think you can do better, my dear chap, you're welcome to try."

The twilit sky darkened, and thunderheads loomed in the west. Reith and Mjipa confronted Barré's entire force in formation. Reith's eleven tourists stood in a clump to one side.

"Friends," began Reith, "we are privileged to attend a service of the Lords of Light, the most exalted of all my world's many faiths and the only one that is perfectly true. I present to you, in gratitude and humility, His Reverence, Bishop Panikkar, to whom I turn over the proceedings."

"Dearly beloved friends," began Mjipa in flawless

178

Durou, "I am here to tell you the tale of the true messenger of God, the martyr Tallal Homsi. Born in humble surroundings in the land called Syria...."

Mjipa retold the story of the founder of the sect, embroidering on the tale that Reith had heard from Ganesh Kosambi. Where the official version gave Homsi credit for only three miracles, Mjipa expanded this to a dozen.

Heavy clouds blotted out the stars. A flicker of lavender lightning preceded a roll of thunder. Mjipa said:

"Now, friends, we come to the most vital part of our ritual. You must follow my directions exactly. When I call *shar pu'án!*, you shall cover your eyes and bow your faces to the earth. I shall pray for one of the Lords of Light to manifest himself. It comes not often to pass; but, when it does come, if your eyes be not covered, you will be blinded by his awful glory. I knew one unfortunate, back on earth, who opened his eyes for the merest blink. The poor wight had thereafter to be led about by a trained animal, called a *dog*, somewhat like unto your eshun. You must not look up until I cry 'Arise!' By then, either our angelic visitor will have departed, or I shall know that he comes not."

With a clatter, Barré's warriors and the chief himself sank to their knees. Mjipa launched into a harangue in a language Reith did not know. A resonant speech with tongue-clicks, Reith guessed it to be Mjipa's native African tongue. At last, Mjipa paused and cried:

"Shar pu'án!"

Barré and his men bowed their faces to the ground and covered their eyes. Mjipa picked up the trumpet and nodded to Reith, who beat the drum. Mjipa began playing his tune on the trumpet. Reith looked towards his tourists and said, as loudly as he dared:

"Go! Damn it, go!"

He and Mjipa were making so much noise that the

tourists did not at first catch on. Then they scrambled up and ran towards the bishtars. The mahouts had turned the animals around, so that they faced the trail back towards Gha'id.

"Keep on, Percy!" panted Reith, banging his drum harder than ever.

The pair continued to play until the last tourist was halfway up his rope ladder. Then, with a mutual nod, they ran for the animals.

Reith's bishtar was already in motion when Reith reached it. He grabbed for a ladder, missed, grabbed again, and was jerked off his feet and dragged. For an instant he thought he would be swept under the elephantine feet and squashed. The first raindrops fell.

Reith hauled himself clear of the ground. The bishtar's speed increased, so that Reith found himself swinging like a clock pendulum at the end of the rope ladder. In climbing, he got his sword entangled in the rope. He had to hold a rung with one hand while he freed the weapon with the other.

"Come on up, Fearless!" Valerie Mulroy called down.

"I'm trying, damn it!" he called back.

The rain came harder. From Barré's camp was heard a shout, then a chorus of yells.

Reith hauled himself into the howdah. He pushed his way aft, where lay his bag.

"Oh, God damn!" he said.

"What's the matter?" said someone.

"We're supposed to be second in line. Just a minute."

Although Barré's camp was now out of sight, a rising volume of sound told Reith that the Ziruma were organizing pursuit. On ayas, they could easily overtake the lumbering bishtars.

Reith worked his way to the front of the howdah

and shouted to the mahout: "Pull over to the side and stop! We must let the others past."

The Krishnan, who had raised an umbrella over his head, ignored the command. Reith shook him by the shoulder and repeated his command.

"I dare not," said the mahout. "The Ziruma would catch and slay us all!"

"Do as I command!" yelled Reith.

"I cannot. I am afraid—"

Holding the edge of the howdah with one hand, Reith drew his sword with the other. "By Qondyor's iron prick, do what I tell you or I'll take off your head!" He touched the side of the Krishnan's neck with his blade.

Grumbling, the mahout obeyed. In the howdah behind Reith, Considine cried: "Hey, Fearless, what are you stopping for? You'll get us caught again, you damned fool!" A crash of thunder drowned out his next words.

"Shut up!" said Reith. Waving frantically in the dark, he called: "Go on, Percy! I've got to bring up the rear!"

The second bishtar tramped past, its huge feet squilching in the mud. Reith could barely make out the beast and its riders.

"Now go again," he told the mahout. "Stay close behind the other."

Reith sheathed his sword, went back to the rear, and took up his bag. He fumbled with the knot in the draw string, which, wet from the rain, refused to untie.

From back up the trail came the rumble of hooves, the clatter of weapons, the creak of harness, and commanding shouts.

"You've got us killed for sure this time!" wailed Turner.

Reith drew his sword again and cut the string. He

dropped the weapon to the floor, reached into the bag, and drew out a caltrop. This consisted of four iron spikes, each six or seven centimeters long. All four were welded together at the base, so that their points made a tetrahedron or triangular pyramid. Hence, when the object was dropped, it always landed standing on the points of three spikes with the fourth sticking straight up. The blacksmith of Gha'id and his sons had worked day and night to complete Reith's order for a hundred and fifty of these devices.

Reith began tossing caltrops over the bishtar's rump. The sounds of pursuit grew louder.

"What are you doing?" asked a tourist.

Reith ignored the question and continued to throw caltrops on the trail behind. Valerie Mulroy said:

"Oh, now I see why you had to be at the tail of the procession."

"Nice to know somebody had a brain," gritted Reith, still tossing caltrops.

The sounds of pursuit continued to wax. Then the tone of the voices changed. Something, beyond the curtain of rain, had interrupted the chase.

Reith threw his last caltrop. The sounds of the Ziruma did not seem to be getting any closer.

"They're to cripple the ayas," Reith explained. "The poor beasts step on them and get a spike through the foot. Then they become unruly and buck off their riders."

"How cruel!" said Shirley Waterford. "How could you, Fearless?"

"I don't like cruelty to animals either; but would you rather go back to Barré's camp?"

Nothing more was said. The tourists huddled under the driving rain, through which the bishtars stolidly tramped. Sounds of pursuit died away.

• • •

The Hostage of Zir

Shortly after noon the next day, the two bishtars shambled into the railroad base camp. Reith was encouraged by the smart way the Duro troops manned the stockade, crossbows ready. They took care to identify the arrivals before admitting them. If Barré mounted a retaliatory attack, he would have a tough nut to crack.

Eleven bedraggled tourists, plus Reith and Mjipa, climbed down the ladders. Lund and Strachan came out to congratulate the fugitives. Strachan said:

"When you didn't arrive early this morning, we were sure Barré had murdered the lot of you."

"Sure, it's taken us a long time to get here," said Reith. "Our mahouts got lost several times. Can't say I blame them, between the rain and the darkness."

"Didna Barré send his men after you on foot, when he found you'd mined the trail?"

Reith shrugged. "If he did, they never caught up with us. Maybe they got lost, too. You can't keep up with a bishtar afoot anyway. Can you have a train to Baianch for us in an hour or two?"

"What's the hurry, laddie? We'd like to hear your people's stories. It gets monotonous out here after the novelty's worn off."

"We've got to shove, Ken. Barré may come down on you, and it's my job to keep my geese out of the fighting."

"If the bandit king does, we shall need all the help we can get."

"Sorry. Maybe a couple of my people, besides myself, might be of some use in a fight. The others would only get in the way."

Strachan sighed. "Well, what must be, must be, as one of their native philosophers put it. I'll make you up a special train."

As the party, lugging baggage, climbed aboard the special, Aimée Jussac asked: "Mr. Mjipa, what was the

183

tune you played on that—that *clairon*, whatever you call it in English?"

"An old Australian song called *Waltzing Matilda*," said Mjipa.

"Ah! I took it for von Suppé's *Light Cavalry Overture*."

Mjipa laughed. "My dear Monsieur Jussac, that proves one of two things. Either I'm no musician, or you have no ear for music. On the whole, I think the former the more likely."

XII.

THE RESTIVE CONSORT

Back in Baianch, Fergus Reith first saw his tourists settled in the Old Palace. Then he went to pay his respects to the Regent.

At the end of his report, he was bidden again to a private supper. At the appointed time, he presented himself in Duro court dress at the door of the private dining chamber. The Regent greeted him warmly, wringing his hand. He said:

"I must apologize, Master Reese. Business of state demands my time, so I shall miss the pleasure of hearing your adventures. From what I'm told, these are worthy of the pen of a Saqqiz or a Harian. The brigand chief is on the move, and we must plan how best to counter him. I leave you to the mercies of my spoilt young kinswoman."

Tashian bowed himself out, leaving Reith alone in the room, except for the guards, with Vázni bad-Dushta'en, Douri of Dur. The princess sat on the far

side of the supper table. Reith's eyes bugged as he took
in her costume. This was a formal dress in Gozashtandou style. It had a long emerald-green skirt but left the
breasts bare, somewhat like the dresses of ancient
Crete. Jewels blazed on her neck, wrists, and brow.

"Like you it?" she said, rising and pirouetting.

"It leaves me speechless," said Reith.

"We wear such fripperies not oft in this cool clime;
but for once I was fain to appear as one of the great
ladies of the more cultivated southerly courts. I'm told
the sight of a woman's milk glands stimulates the males
of your species. Be that sooth?"

Reith gulped. "It affects me for certain, Douri."

"Strange; 'tis not the case with us." She poured kvad
for both. "Still, I'm glad my appearance titillates you.
What true female would not wish every male to lust
after her on sight? Tell me, does my aspect impas-
sionate you as much as would that of one of your
terran dames?"

"If it impassionated me any more—well, my lady, I
know not what to say. I try to stay within the bounds of
courtly manners."

She giggled. "Most excellently put, Master Reese! I
take your meaning and rejoice in your unspoken
thoughts. With me, alas, such things have perforce
been kept on the plane of thought, for my tyrannous
cousin has allowed me no lover or husband. But now
tell me of your latest escape. You must, ere you depart
our demesne, dictate the tale to one of our scriveners.
Our poets shall make it into an heroic lay."

Glad to have the conversation take a less perilous
turn, Reith launched into his story. By concentrating
on flights, pursuits, and close calls, he managed to
forget the pounding of his pulse. He was still talking
when supper was cleared away.

"Come to my sitting room," said Vázni, "where we

shan't have these honest yokels of guards breathing down our necks."

She led him into the sitting room into which he had blundered that earler time, when he had gotten drunk playing piza with Strachan. She rang a little bell on the table, and a serving girl brought another jug and goblets. Pouring, Vázni said:

"Master Reese, I've heard that among earthmen, you have two names apiece."

"At least two," said Reith. "Three is usual. My full name is Fergus MacNairn Reith."

"And they say you use the second name—I mean the last name—for formal occasions but the first among intimates. Be that right?"

"Aye, Douri. Customs, howsomever, differ. In my America, we use the first name on short acquaintance."

"'Tis otherwise amongst us. Now, my true and only name is Vázni. The bad-Dushta'en means merely offspring of Dushta'en. Now let's leave these philological quibbles. May I call you Fergus?" She pronounced it "fair-goss."

"I shall be honored, Douri."

"'Twere easier than your other, which ends in a hissing sound I cannot frame. And you shall call me Vázni. Go on with your tale, Fergus. You were sliding down the trail in the dark and storm on the backs of those bishtars."

Fergus told his story. He had now drunk enough kvad so that his head spun a little. He stifled a yawn.

"Naughty, naughty!" said Vázni, wagging a finger. "But, sooth to say, I, too, wax sleepy. Yet I'll not forgo the rest of your tale of feats that overpass the Six Labors of Qarar. I know what!"

She rang the bell again. When the maid appeared, Vázni whispered to her. The girl hurried away, and Vázni rose.

"Come," she said. "I've made sure we shan't be disturbed."

Taking Reith's hand, she led him into her bedroom. Inside, she closed the door, faced Reith, and slid her hands up his arms. They kissed.

From then on, everything seemed to happen without volition, as in a dream. Reith was hardly aware of buttons and snaps; their garments seemed to flow off them as if somehow liquefied. Vázni's jewels littered the rug.

They walked to the bed with neither haste nor hesitation, as if they had long known each other. Entry was as easy as that of a key into a well-oiled lock.

Reith was relaxing afterwards. Looking up from the pillow, Vázni said: "Fergus dear, what's that little pit in the center of your belly? Is't a scar from some wound?"

"Oh, you mean my navel, as we call it. You egg-layers don't have them, do you? It has to do with—"

A deep voice said: "Well, well, sirrah! I trust you've found my cousin's hospitality to your liking?"

Tashian, sword in hand, had entered the bedroom. Four armed guards followed him. The huge Regent wore the Krishnan version of a grin.

Reith made a strangled sound. There flashed through his head the Krishnan legend of the lovers Sivandi and Zerré. The latter had rescued the former from captivity by the giant Damghan. In their flight, however, they stopped to make love. Catching them *in coitu*, the giant had pinned both to the earth with a single thrust of his spear. Reith wondered if Tashian had something of the sort in mind. A naked man in his present posture was about as defenseless as one could be.

"Well, get up!" said Tashian. "You cannot lie there all night, and we have tasks to perform."

Reith, who had been paralyzed with dismay,

separated himself from Vázni. "Ouch!" he said as he planted a bare foot on one of Vázni's jeweled ornaments on the floor.

"Look not so fearful, earthman," continued Tashian. "I intend no murder or mutilation. Happily, there's a less sanguinary way to repair the harm you've done our family's honor, if you but do as required."

"May—may I don my garments?"

"Certes! 'Twere clean against custom to wed naked, as do the savages of Zhamanak. You, too, Vázni."

"Oh, Tashian!" said Vázni. "Mean you that?" Reith thought she looked entirely too pleased.

"Certes," said the Regent. "I generally mean what I say, saving matters of diplomacy."

"Mean you he shall be all mine?"

"Aye, little fluff-head. Finish your dressing, Master Reese. Oh, Father Khorsh! They're decent. Come in."

The priest said: "Good-even, Master Reese. 'Tis a goodly while since I've had the pleasure of your company. Now, I understand, you and the Douri are fain to wed?"

"Uk," said Reith, his eyes on the five naked swords.

"That's 'aye' in one of those terran tongues," said Tashian.

"And you, my lady?"

"With all my liver," said Vázni.

"Very well, then." The priest went into a long prayer to Bákh, which Reith could not follow because it was in Old Varastou. Khorsh shot questions at the pair, to which Reith mumbled replies and Vázni gave clear ones. At last the priest said:

"And now, by the authority vested in me, I declare that under the laws of Dur and the blessing of the immortal gods, Reese and Vázni are wedded, so to remain until severed by death or divorce. Love each other; support each other in adversity; bear and forbear."

Khorsh produced a paper covered with hooks and curlycues. Although Reith could not read it, he signed where indicated. Vázni also signed.

Khorsh intoned another archaic prayer and gave a blessing. Tashian handed the priest a golden coin. Khorsh thanked him, put the money in the wallet at his belt, bowed to Reith and Vázni, and went out.

"So, beloved cousin-by-marriage," said Tashian, "a few simple words have enrolled you among the great ones of this mighty empire, as well as made you the consort of my shapely cousin. You might as well relax and enjoy your lot. Think not to slip away, either. You'll be closely watched. Should you rashly essay to flee, know that there's an island, called Pák, where I keep subjects whose freedom is dangerous to the state. None has ever escaped it."

"But—but my tourists!" cried Reith. "I'm responsible for getting them back to Novo."

"That shall be taken care of. Khorsh will guide them."

"He speaks no English and they no Portuguese."

"Then they must needs use sign language. And now good-night. Pleasant dreams!"

Tashian and the guards went out. Vázni said: "Is't not wonderful, Fergus? Long have I dreamed of an heroic husband, but my cousin has fended off all suitors. And now I have the most heroic husband of all, who can also stroke me a mighty stroke! 'Twas all I'd dreamed of; let's do it again!"

"I see nought heroic about getting out of a few tight fixes I shouldn't have gotten into in the first place," said Reith. "As for more love-making, I fear you must wait until morn. The night's events have sapped my heroic vigor. How can I get my gear from the Old Palace? I need at least my toothbrush."

"I'll send a servant for your things. Oh, darling, we shall be so happy!"

We shall see about that, thought Reith.

Five days later, Kenneth Strachan entered the room in the New Palace that had been turned over to Reith for his private study. Reith was frowning over a Duro grammar, trying to master the written form. A sheet of paper, covered with his squiggles, lay on the table.

"Ken!" he cried. "How did you get in? They've been keeping me away from all other earthmen."

Strachan grinned. "I walked. The guards all knew me and let me by from force of habit. These folk are amusing, but efficient they are not."

"How'd you hear where I was?"

"I saw your tourists off on the *Sárbez* this morning. Not seeing you among them, I asked about. I suppose I ought to congratulate you."

"Or commiserate. It wasn't my idea." In a few words, Reith told of his forced marriage.

Strachan suppressed a chuckle. "You silly stirk! Don't you see what Tashian's doing? He wants to make sure Vázni bears no legitimate egg. If she hatches a male chick and it grows up, that's the end of his power. He's sure he's the only one who can modernize and consolidate this great, sprawling empire, divided by feuds among feudal families, fanatical sects, tribal rivalries, bloodthirsty revolutionaries, class conflict, and everything else you can think of. He may be right about that.

"Up to now, he's sent Vázni's suitors packing, however rich or high-born or able. Vázni's a hot little piece who wants a good stroking, but he makes sure she disna get it. Then come you, the answer to his prayer. If he marries her to you, there'll be no egg, since he knows you and she are intersterile.

"He also knows you're no threat to his power, since a foreigner—and even more a non-Krishnan—could never enlist a personal following. Tony Fallon got away with it for a while on Zamba, but those were the days when you could fool the Krishnans by disguising yourself as one. So Tashy lays a trap, and you walk blindly into it."

"I thought there must be some such reason, but I was too dumb to see it."

"How do you find her? D'ye love the lassie?"

"I like her; wouldn't say loved. She's pretty, even by our standards, and good-natured, with a certain girlish charm. She's also a hell of a good lay. Trouble is, she wants it every night and morning. I think my endowments are normal, but I'm not quite up to such an exacting schedule. Also, she's a flutter-wit and none too bright. My God, she's dull! Next to lovemaking, she thinks mostly about clothes. After an hour with her, I'm bored and looking for an excuse to get away."

"Weel, as the Krishnans say, count not the teeth of a gift shomal. Many a man finds a stupid wife just the ticket. Makes him feel big to do the thinking for both."

"Not this *Ertsu*. I want to find my dream girl, settle down on good old earth, and have kids."

Strachan shrugged. "Puir Fergus! Every female with a hot notch in her crotch makes a set for you. It must be that beautiful red hair."

"Very flattering, but I could do with less flattery."

"If you had an unco' stiff yard, you should ha' come with me. I'd have seen you were fucked out, so you wunda fall into the royal family's trap."

"It was that topless dress that did me in. Still, I doubt if Vázni knew what the Regent was up to. She hasn't the brains—"

"Na, na, she just did what came naturally. But you're not faring badly here." Strachan glanced around.

"I've had my bellyful of what passes for luxury on Krishna. I don't like even the fanciest jail, especially one without electricity, running water, or central heating."

"You roughed it well enough in Zir."

"That's different. This sort of thing is okay for a visit but not for a life sentence."

Strachan lowered his voice. "Have you thought of escaping? You got away from Barré and Shosti."

"You bet I've thought of it! But Tashian's thought of it, too. He has me watched night and day."

"This episode won't do Tashy's tourism any good."

"I told him that, but he just waved it off. Said if anything it would encourage tourism. I'd be his star attraction once I realized how lucky I was and settled down."

"I know. He told your trippers you and Vázni were so madly in love he was forced to give in, and you'd decided to spend the rest of your life in Dur. Fact is, he likes the tourist trade, but he likes his power even more.

"Weel, keep your courage up, man. The Regent may die, or Vázni may die, or you may die. In either case, you'll be free of your gilded cage. Now I'm off for Gha'id."

"Give my best to Siggy."

The three satellites of Krishna—Karrim, Golnaz, and Sheb—continued to orbit the planet. Little by little, as Reith played the devoted, contented consort, the restrictions upon him relaxed. He followed the tactics that had worked with the Witch of Zir.

He attended state dinners, where he found that Krishnan orators could say even less in more words than those on earth. He went to diplomatic parties, where he discovered that those who had interesting inside information would say nothing about it, so that people talked of their houses, their children, their servants, their incomes, and their aches and pains. He officially opened a new bridge to traffic by cutting a rope across it with his sword.

He sat by the hour watching Vázni try on dresses brought to the palace by eager merchants. He felt some sympathy for the Regent. Vázni had bought so many garments on credit that, at her present clothing allowance, it would take years to pay for the clothes she already had.

Reith was reminded that his own ready cash would not last forever, even though he was eating free and spending little. He asked the Regent:

"Your Excellency, as royal consort, shouldn't I, too, receive a regular wage?"

"That you should, my lord Fergus." (Tashian pronounced it "fog-gas.") "As soon as our present problems of state grant me the leisure to think on't, I'll arrange a stipend."

Although Reith renewed his request every few days thereafter, Tashian was always too busy to attend to the matter. The Regent did, however, find time to elevate Reith to knighthood—a rank that had become purely ornamental in Dur. Reith did not mind being addressed as "Garm" or "Sir" Fergus; but he would really have preferred an assured income, even a small one.

For the present, he managed for drink and sundries money by selling one of the emeralds from the girdle of his Senarzé temple costume. When these gave out, he wondered, would he have to hunt a job, say as a teacher of terran languages?

One evening, suitably guarded, he attended a play with Vázni. This was a revival of Harian's *The Conspirators*, in five acts and twenty-two scenes. He started to read a metrical romance, *Abbeq and Danqi*, in the original Gozashtandou. But he never got through more than a few of its 264 cantos, finding Duro spelling almost as erratic as that of English.

He wheedled from Tashian permission to walk abroad in Baianch, accompanied by four stalwart guardsmen. Then the Regent, ever alert for ways to cut expenses, reduced the escort to two and finally to one, an amiable but simple-minded young Duru named Tázád.

Reith explored the city as thoroughly as he had Senarzé, tramping down the slopes to the lower city and back up until his escorts complained of exhaustion. He borrowed scooters from the royal stables and, with his escorts, went bumping over the cobbles of Baianch.

One day, Reith and Tázád came out of a grog shop on the waterfront. Sitting on a bollard at the edge of the wharf, below the frowning gray battlements of the upper town, Reith said:

"*Ohé*, what's that yonder?"

He pointed to a vessel anchored out in the shimmering bay. This ship differed greatly from the usual Va'andao square-rigger.

"That?" said Tázád. "Means Your Lordship that black craft with the tall pipe in the middle?" Tázád had a habit of making a questioner repeat every question.

"Aye, lad."

"That, Sir Fergus, hight the *Mokinam*, a ship of the Prince of Sotaspé."

"I thought I knew her," mused Reith. "I've seen her before at Reshr."

"They say she's driven by a magical spell, the which Prince Ferrian stole from the earthmen," said Tázád. "The priests warn us against such things, saying they're worked with the aid of evil spirits."

"What does Prince Ferrian here?"

"Mean, ye, Sir Fergus, on what business visits he Dur?"

"Certes."

"Well, sir, I know not truly the secrets of the great. Your Altitude were better fitted than I to hear. They say he be here on some mission to His Excellence but dare not come ashore, lest Lord Tashian clap him up in prison. So the Regent's man is busy all day, being rowed back and forth betwixt ship and shore, to carry the details of their chaffer."

"Interesting," said Reith, staring at the steamship. "Let's have another drink." Perhaps he could make Tázád insensible as he had the unfortunate Captain Parang.

Tázád said: "May it please Your Lordship, I'll watch whilst ye drink but will decline the offer. My commander strictly charged me to stay sober."

Reith grunted. Just his luck, to have so conscientious a Krishnan for watchdog! He took Tázád into the drink shop, ordered two kvads, and tried to tempt the Duru with one of them. Tázád, politely respectful, proved adamant. Not daring to put on enough pressure to arouse suspicion, Reith ended by drinking both mugs himself.

Two days later, the *Mokinam* was still at anchor. Although Tashian had tried to insulate Reith from the levers of power, Reith still managed to coax information of Ferrian's visit from the Duruma whom he knew around the palaces. Krishnans were great gossips.

The visit, Reith learned, was not going well. Ferrian was constructing a federation of the islands of the Sadabao Sea; his own Sotaspé, Zamba, Jerud, Zá, Ulvanagh, and the rest. He wanted trading privileges for this confederacy in the Va'andao Sea, which the navy of Dur now barred to non-Duro ships. Tashian, on the other hand, would relax his monopoly of Va'andao shipping only on terms that virtually made the Sadabao Isles a Duro protectorate.

They said the negotiations were doomed to break down any day. From the waterfront, Reith gazed longingly at Prince Ferrian's ship. Once the *Mokinam* steamed away, Bákh only knew when Reith would get another chance to flee. The day was warm, sunny, and windless, with scarcely a wave on the blue-green sea.

As Reith watched, a disturbance broke out on the waterfront. Someone was beating a fire gong. Smoke poured from a ship chandler's shop.

"*Ohé*, a fire!" cried Tázád. "Let's lend a hand with the buckets, Your Altitude!"

The guardsman ran towards the fire. Reith followed more slowly. Others converged on the scene. A whistle blew, and a squad of firemen jogged around a corner, pushing their engine. This was a large, empty wooden tub, piled with buckets, on wheels. A long-handled pump with a pivoted nozzle rose from the tub.

Shouting to make way, the firemen halted the apparatus in front of the burning shop. They handed out buckets to the gathering crowd, who formed a double line from the shop to the bay and back again. The linesmen passed empty buckets along one line and those filled with sea water back along the other. As the full buckets arrived at the engine, they were emptied into the tub. Firemen heaved on the pump handles, and a jet of water shot into the shop. Oblivious to Reith, Tázád was hard at work in one of the bucket lines.

Reith took a place at the seaward end of the empty-bucket line. He took buckets, leaned over the edge of the wharf, filled each bucket, and handed it to the end man of the other line. It was hot work.

"*Ohé*, bean't ye that earthman who married the Douri?" said a nearby Krishnan.

"The same," panted Reith. "Here, you take my place for a spell." Reith stepped aside to peel off his tunic and shirt.

"Good for you!" said the Krishnan. "'Tis good to see Your Lordship's not too high and mighty to help us poor folk—*Iyá!* What do ye?"

Freed of tunic and shirt, Reith glanced at Tázád. The guardsman had his back to him. Off went Reith's shoes and trousers, leaving him in his underwear. Under his underwear, next to his skin, he wore the emerald-studded girdle from his Senarzean temple costume. Standing on the edge of the wharf, he dove off.

He came up sputtering in oily water. Garbage and other débris, including a dead eshun, bobbed on the ripples. Reith avoided the carcass and struck out for the *Mokinam*.

A plume of blue smoke arose from the tall, thin stack of the ship. The sight spurred Reith to swim harder. The black ship might be leaving.

A glance behind showed several Krishnans in a cluster on the wharf, looking towards him. At this distance, Reith could not tell if one was Tázád. Most of the crowd were still concentrating on the fire.

Lack of breath forced Reith to slow down. The last hundred meters he made with a breast stroke as least tiring.

As Reith neared the ship, there were shouts of command and signs of activity. The anchor rope started to rise through the hawsehole.

"Hey!" called Reith, getting a mouthful of brackish water.

With a last effort, he swam to the anchor rope and seized it. Above, he could hear a chantey as the sailors walked the capstan round.

The rope continued to rise, pulling Reith out of the water. He locked his legs around the rope to relieve the strain on his arms. A meter below him, the anchor broke the surface.

Soon, Reith saw, he would have to let go to avoid having his hands jammed between the rope and the rim of the hawsehole. Watching the approach of the aperture, he waited until his hands were only centimeters from the hole. Releasing the rope, he grabbed the gunwale. He tried to hoist himself up to the rail but could not; his arms were too exhausted.

"Help!" he called. "Help! In the bow!"

Bare feet slapped the deck. A couple of weathered Krishnan faces looked over the rail. There was a rattle of speech, and a rope was dropped over the side within reach.

Reith grasped the rope with his remaining strength. The rope was drawn up until he could reach the rail. With horny hands grasping his arms to help, he tumbled over the rail and collapsed on the deck.

"Well, sir," said a Krishnan voice in excellent English, "When we had our little fencing bout in Reshr, I never thought to fish you out of the sea like this. What in the name of all your terran gods are you doing here?"

Prince Ferrian, booted and scarlet-sashed, stood before Reith with a hand on the jeweled hilt of his sword.

"I'm glad you remember me," said Reith.

"I always remember faces. But how about answering my question?"

"It's a long story, sir, and I'm out of breath. I'll just say that the Regent was holding me prisoner, and I escaped."

"What had you done to earn his ire?"

"Nothing. He picked me as a consort for the Douri and framed me into marrying her."

"Really? Many would think you lucky; but tastes differ, especially as between Krishnans and terrans. What became of your tourists?"

"They've gone back to Novo, I hope."

Staring shoreward, Ferrian said: "Your escape seems to have been noticed. Here comes a boat with Tashian's flag in the bow."

"Please, Prince, don't send me back!"

"Why shouldn't I, Mr.—what's your name again?"

"Fergus Reith."

"Mr. Reith. One earthman means nothing to me, compared to the good of my realm. Neither have I much prejudice in favor of your species. Why should I rile Tashian more than I must?"

"I hear your negotiations with him have broken down."

"True, but that doesn't alter matters. Besides, if I don't give you up, Tashian could come out and take you by force. He might grab me and my ship and crew in the bargain."

"Can't you just steam away?" asked Reith.

"Alas, no. I meant to, but something's wrong with my damned engine. It won't turn the paddle wheels. I have sails, but they're no good in this flat calm."

The approaching wherry was close enough for Reith to make out the scarlet yeki on the languidly flapping flag. A hail came across the water, and Ferrian stepped to the rail.

"What is it?" he shouted through a speaking trumpet.

"The Douri's consort, an earthman, has fled to your ship, my lord. Give him to us."

"Stall, Prince!" said Reith. "Tell him you'll give him an answer later."

Ferrian cracked a small smile. "Grant me an hour to sift the facts, gentles," he called. He turned to Reith. "What's your plan, Mr. Reith?"

The Krishnan in the bow of the wherry shouted back: "Nay, good my lord! The Regent demands this Reese creature forthwith!"

"I can fix your engine," said Reith.

"Are you an engineer?"

"No, but I had to learn about such things when I taught school."

Ferrian turned back to the boat. "I said, you shall have him when I have learned all the facts, and not before!"

"I bear the Regent's command!" shrieked the Krishnan in the boat. "Lower the ladder at once, on pain of his displeasure!"

"You heard me," replied Ferrian. "You shall have him ere sunset. That's that."

"You shall rue your contumely!" yelled the Duru. The boat swung round had headed back towards the pier.

"Very well, Mr. Reith," said Ferrian. "If you can repair my balky engine, you'd better do so pretty damned quick."

"In this calm," said Reith, "how could Tashian's sailing ships sail out to attack you?"

"They couldn't, but he has a couple of galleys for such contingencies. He doesn't use them often, because these waters are too stormy and they have poor sea-keeping ability. It'll take time to round up the rowers, too. But you'd better get going, as you Americans say."

Below, Reith found the Krishnan engineer puttering distractedly among the pipes and shafts and connecting rods. When Reith asked him for particulars, the Krishnan replied in so strong a dialect of Gozashtandou that Reith could not understand. He had to beg Ferrian to come down to translate.

Firewood blazed merrily in the furnace; water bubbled in the boiler. The safety valve opened with a shrill hiss, sent out clouds of vapor for half a minute, and then closed again. But the crankshaft turned not.

Reith went over the machinery, trying to remember the diagrams and texts of the children's books of science, with which he had once been familiar. The engine was a simple two-cylinder, single-expansion reciprocating steam engine, of a type virtually extinct on earth outside museums of technology.

Reith could find no leaks in the piping. The main cylinder packing seemed to be in order. He could find nothing wrong with the eccentrics. What in heaven's name could ail so simple a machine and not be obvious to even a non-expert like himself?

A crewman called down the ladder. Prince Ferrian said: "Excuse me, Mr. Reith. They tell me the galleys are coming out. Tashian's manned them more quickly than I expected."

The prince scrambled back up the ladder. The safety valve continued to pop at intervals, making the air steamy. Reith wiped the sweat out of his eyes and went over the engine again. Could the crankshaft bearings have seized up? They looked all right, but one would have to disassemble the connecting rods to be sure.

"Goodman Hurgash," he said to the engineer, "where's your starting rod?"

"Yonder," said the Krishnan, pointing to a crowbarlike rod in a bracket on the wall.

"Let's give her a twist to see if the paddles turn." Reith got down the bar and thrust it between the spokes of the flywheel. With both heaving on the pole, they made the crankshaft and paddle wheels do a quarter turn.

"She turns easily enough," mused Reith. "So 'tis not the bearings. But where's the power loss?"

The Krishnan made a helpless gesture. Ferrian called down: "You have but a few minutes, Mr. Reith, before the galleys arrive. I shan't try to fight them. With all those rowers, who double as deck fighters, they outnumber us ten to one."

Reith went over the mechanism again. Then he said: "Hurgash! What's this?"

He pointed to a flyball governor on the main steam pipe. He could not understand the engineer's reply, but it made no difference. He remembered that one of the children's books told how the great James Watt invented the device. Reith had overlooked the governor because it rose from a section of the main steam pipe in shadow.

The governor was in the closed position, with its balls at maximum extension and legs nearly horizontal. Reith crawled up, to where he could reach it, yelping "Ouch!" as a hot pipe burned his hand.

"A tool, Hurgash! Something wherewith to pry!"

The engineer handed Reith a screwdriver. Reith thrust the tool into the legs of the governor and pried. The lower bearing sleeve of the governor came down stickily. There was a loud hiss from the steam pipe; the governor began to spin and, much more slowly, the crankshaft to turn.

"I've got it, Prince!" yelled Reith. "You didn't clean your governor. The oil dried up and got sticky, so she somehow jammed in the closed position. Hand me the oil can, Hurgash!"

Faster went the crankshaft. The ship shuddered to the sound of paddles striking water. Reith scrambled up the ladder.

On deck, sailors rushed about to obey Ferrian's commands. They were setting wicker shields along the rail and pulling a catapult into position on the quarterdeck.

The *Mokinam* gathered speed. Astern, the two Duro galleys, like gigantic centipedes, foamed in her wake. The shouts and gong notes of the coxswains came across the water.

"Down!" cried Ferrian, dropping to the deck. His sailors did likewise. Something went *whang* on one of the galleys. Reith was just beginning to prostrate himself when a catapult dart screeched overhead.

203

"If you're as slow as that you may lose your head next time," said the prince, rising. "They're still gaining."

Centimeter by centimeter, the Duro galleys crept closer. Ferrian said: "Good try, Mr. Reith, but I fear we must heave to. I'm sorry."

"Wait!" said Reith. "They haven't gained in the last minute."

"Wishful thinking, my dear fellow. . . . I say, you may be right at that! Their rowers can't last long at that pace. That's the big advantage of steam power over muscle: steam doesn't get tired."

Another catapult dart came whistling, to bury its head in the deck planking.

"They're dropping back," said Reith. "I'll bet my head on it."

Another dart fell into the water astern.

"See what I mean?" said Reith.

As their rowers became exhausted, the galleys went slower and slower. The *Mokinam* plodded ahead.

"Wow!" shouted Reith. "They're turning back."

Ferrian shut the brass spyglass with which he had been watching the pursuers. "You win point, set, and match, Mr. Reith." In Gozashtandou he called: "Master Pasháu, set course for the Strait of Uporé!" Then back to Reith: "Let's go to my cabin. We might have a bit of business to discuss."

Into the Novo Iorque Bar stepped Fergus Reith. His costume was that of a Krishnan sailor, including a brass-hilted cutlass at his hip. His face was red and his nose was peeling.

In the bar, little Herculeu Castanhoso sat at a table, playing a samba tune on a recorder. A small dance floor had been cleared, and there four couples danced. There were Percy Mjipa and his massive black wife, Kenneth Strachan and a Krishnan female, Sigvard

Lund and another female Krishnan, and Ivar Heggstad with one of the terran girls who worked at Novorecife. To Castanhoso's Brazilian tune they were doing a Scandinavian folk dance, with stamping, hand-clapping, and kissing.

Strachan glanced at the doorway and stopped dancing. Eyes wide, he cried: "Heuch, man, will ye look what's come in! It's aul' Fergus or his ghaist!"

There was a stampede to greet Reith. Strachan said: "Every time we think poor Fergus is gone for good, he turns up alive. How do you do it?"

Reith said: "I can't help it if I've become the greatest escape artist since that fellow Houdunnit, or whatever his name was. These nutty things happen to me, and I have to get out of them as best I can."

They urged him to the table. Castanhoso said: "You have been sunburned lately."

"Yes, cruising on Prince Ferrian's steamship. We redheads don't tan well."

"We heard he had replaced the *Kerukchi*," said Castanhoso. "But tell us of your latest exploits. We thought you were settled in Baianch as the Douri's pampered consort."

Reith gave a brief account of his escape.

"By feigs, man!" said Strachan. "When your tourists called you 'Fearless,' they weren't altogether joking."

"Don't tell anybody, but I was scared as green as a Krishnan most of the time. Speaking of my geese, what happened to them?"

Mjipa said: "They got back to Novo, but just barely."

"How did they manage for language, since Khorsh had only Portuguese?"

"That wasn't the main problem. Jussac, it turned out, spoke some Portuguese, and Guzmán-Vidal's Spanish was close enough to Khorsh's Brazilian so that they could understand each other somewhat."

"Then what was their trouble?"

"First, Jussac got sick with some stomach ailment."

"No wonder," said Reith, "the way he ate everything in sight. Then?"

"Everything went to pot. When Jussac resigned, Considine and Guzmán-Vidal both wanted to succeed him as leader. They quarreled and intrigued night and day. In Chesht, that black woman—Waterton?—Waterford, Shirley Waterford, almost got them arrested. The local journal sent a reporter for an interview, and as luck would have it, he picked Shirley. She told him all about the rotten socio-economic systems of Krishna. All very true, of course, but that didn't make it sit any better with the Pandr of Lusht when the paper appeared."

"How would you say 'socio-economic' in Gozashtandou?" said Strachan.

"No idea," continued Mjipa. "Then, the Guzmán-Vidals were late for the sailing, and the *Sárbez* went off without them. It was all Khorsh could do to persuade Captain Denaikh to go back for them.

"In Reshr, that ass Pride got into an altercation with some seller of trinkets, neither understanding a word of what the other was saying. The coppers hauled Pride off to jail until Khorsh got him out.

"That night, Considine and Turner got roaring drunk and went around breaking windows. When one of the night watch tried to stop them, they threw him in the canal. It's just luck the chap was fished out before he drowned, or they'd have lost their heads. As it was, the whole gang, including Father Khorsh, were thrown in the *calabouço* until I could come over from Monyisotri and get them out.

"A week in that stinking hole forced a little sense into their heads. They chose Mrs. Whitney Scott leader, and the old girl proved the best man of the lot. I saw them to Novo, and they all went off on the next earth-bound ship except the Guzmán-Vidals and Maurice Considine."

"What about the Guzmán-Vidals?"

"Señora Pilar had got pregnant. They knew they weren't supposed to but ran out of medicine. When I asked Santiago why in hell he couldn't lay off his wife for a while, he gave me his usual guff." Mjipa exaggerated Guzmán-Vidal's accent: "'Ay red-blooded man like me cannot become ay monk all at once! Eet ees against thee nature!' Anyway, they didn't dare leave with the others for fear of the acceleration."

"Where are they now?"

"Here in Novo, awaiting the blessed event."

"And Considine?"

"Funny thing. While waiting here for the flight, he took up with a Krishnan woman in the Hamda'. Turner got jealous, and they had a frightful quarrel and broke up. Turner went home on the ship, sniffling as he boarded it. Considine, who knows enough of the native speech to get by, somehow wangled a job as teacher of sculpture at the University of Hershid. He took the native female with him."

"You mean Maurice has gone hetero?"

Mjipa shrugged. "Looks that way. Maybe Krishnan females affect him in a way that human women don't."

Reith said: "The Gozashtanduma will find him a difficult character. They'd better not let him near their little boys."

"That's their problem. Turner accused the Mulroy woman of leading Maurice down the primrose path. Perhaps she did; she seems to have bloody well tried out everything else with testicles."

"Anyway, Valerie took my part against the other geese a couple of times when I needed all the support I could get, and I'm not ungrateful. For that matter, all of them—except maybe that loon Silvester Pride—had at least some good qualities." Reith turned to

207

Strachan. "How's your railroad, Ken?"

"We're waiting while Tashian and Barré hammer out a treaty for extending the line through Zir. Barré attacked the base camp, as you said he would, but was beaten off with loss. I got one of the bastitches myself, with a sword."

"Up Scotland!" said Reith. "What then?"

"Tashy sent a punitive force into Zir, but Barré ambushed them and killed over half. The Regent had tried to do it on the cheap, as usual. So they decided that, since neither could knock the other out, they'd better seek an agreement."

The door opened, and in came a stocky, flat-featured, black-haired man on crutches. Castanhoso said:

"Mr. Reith, here is a colleague of yours. I present Mr. Wang Tso-liang, of the Middle Kingdom Travel Bureau. Mr. Wang, Mr. Fergus Reith—Sir Fergus, I suppose I should say."

Reith got up and shook hands. "So you fellows got here after all!"

Wang ducked his head. "Yes, sir. It is disappointment that you beat us, but that is a small thing compared to our present misfortune."

"What happened?"

"I am stupid, that is all. On arrival, I was leading my tourists down the ramp, and I fell off and broke leg. Now they are stranded here. Will not be good for me back in China."

"I'm sorry," said Reith. "Won't you be out of your cast in time for their tour?"

Wang sighed. "Doctor says, not for another month, earth time. If I could find substitute—" He broke off, staring at Reith. "Mr. Reith, could you take my party? Arrangements are all made. I will see you are paid what I should have been."

"No sir!" cried Reith. "By God, I've shaken the dust of Krishna from my feet! I'm flattered by your offer, Mr. Wang; but I've had enough close shaves here to last me the rest of my life. Besides, I don't speak Chinese."

"Would not be necessary," said Wang. "I have fourteen Chinese, one Korean, and one Japanese. Mr. Kamimura, Mr. Chien, and Mrs. Li speak excellent English, and most others know a little."

Reith persisted in polite refusals until Wang leaned forward and said earnestly: "Mr. Reith, as you know, in China everything is government. My government allows me to draw on emergency fund, in case some disaster like this happens. If you will take my people, I will commit whole amount to your personal account. We cannot have so great loss of face."

"How much?" said Reith.

"One hundred thousand liang."

Reith stifled an impulse to whistle. "Where were you going?"

"Our itinerary much the same as yours. Majbur, Zamba, Katai-Jhogorai, and Dur."

"You won't get me near Dur!" said Reith. "I'll explain some other time. One could, however, substitute a cruise on the Sadabao, on Prince Ferrian's steamboat, to Varzeni-Ganderan and Sotaspé. Ferrian and I talked about it while he was bringing me to Majbur. He would of course have to be sure you W. F. people wouldn't board and scuttle his ship, the way you did the other."

"He need not worry," said Castanhoso. "We have given up on his ships. The way things are going, what technical information does not leak through the blockade, the Krishnans will find out for themselves. Any day now," he concluded gloomily, "we expect to hear that somebody has invented the gun."

"Go ahead, Fergus," said Strachan. "Back on Terra, that money'll keep you for life. Besides, you're now the ablest and most experienced guide to Krishna alive."

"I can't very well help being, since I'm the only one besides Mr. Wang," said Reith. "But I'm determined to stay alive, too."

Mjipa was filling his pipe. "In fact," he growled, "you're a bloody hero, whether you like it or not. According to your tourists, you're the greatest tour leader since Moses. After what you've been through, you don't have any silly sentimental notions about the natives. You know the blighters for what they are."

"Sure," said Heggstad. "It vould give me a chance to teach you some more fencing, while you are getting your tour organized."

"You," said Lund, breaking his usual silence, "are now the grand old man of Krishnan tour guiding. You might as well put your experience to use."

Reith drew a long breath. "Okay, Mr. Wang; I'll take your tour. My dream girl will have to wait."

"What? I beg pardon?" said Wang.

"Nothing; just a silly thought. I'll say one thing, though. I'd like to catch that guy Otis Burroughs or whatever his name was, who wrote those stories about earthmen who go to other planets and marry native princesses. Too bad he's long dead. I could tell him a thing or two!"

Sit down, relax and read a good book . . .

CURRENT BESTSELLERS FROM BERKLEY

BEYOND JOGGING: (03733-9—$1.50)
The Inner Spaces of Running
  by Mike Spino

THE BOOK OF MERLYN   (03826-2—$2.25)
  by T. H. White

A CHILD IS MISSING   (03833-5—$1.95)
  by Charlotte Paul

THE FIRST DEADLY SIN   (03904-8—$2.50)
  by Lawrence Sanders

GRINDING IT OUT: (03842-4—$1.95)
The Making of McDonald's
  by Ray Kroc with Robert Anderson

THE ONCE AND FUTURE KING (03796-7—$2.75)
  by T. H. White

THE SECOND DEADLY SIN   (03923-4—$2.50)
  by Lawrence Sanders

THE TANGENT OBJECTIVE   (04340-1—$2.25)
  by Lawrence Sanders

Send for a list of all our books in print.

These books are available at your local bookstore, or send
price indicated plus 30¢ for postage and handling. If more
than four books are ordered, only $1.00 is necessary for
postage. Allow three weeks for delivery. Send orders to:

      Berkley Book Mailing Service
      P.O. Box 690
      Rockville Centre, New York 11570

"WE ONLY HAVE ONE TEXAS"

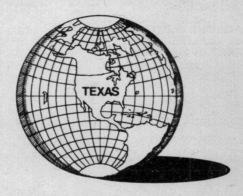

People ask if there is really an energy crisis. Look at it this way. World oil consumption is 60 million barrels per day and is growing 5 percent each year. This means the world must find three million barrels of new oil production each day. Three million barrels per day is the amount of oil produced in Texas as its peak was 5 years ago. The problem is that it is not going to be easy to find a Texas-sized new oil supply every year, year after year. In just a few years, it may be impossible to balance demand and supply of oil unless we start conserving oil today. So next time someone asks: "is there really an energy crisis?" Tell them: "yes, we only have one Texas."

ENERGY CONSERVATION -
IT'S YOUR CHANCE TO SAVE, AMERICA

Department of Energy, Washington, D.C.

Published in Australia 2017
by New Frontier Publishing Pty Ltd
ABN 67 126 171 757
48 Ross Street, Glebe NSW 2037, Australia
www.newfrontier.com.au

A Cataloging-in-Publication entry for this
book is available from the National Library of Australia.
ISBN: 978-1-925059-98-4

Designed by Celeste Hulme

Printed in China
10 9 8 7 6 5 4 3 2 1

For Luke, forever a light in my heart. AR

For Dad, Mum and Valeria, with all my love. AP

AVA'S
spectacular
SPECTACLES

Alice Rex & Angela Perrini

Ava sat at her desk, gazing at the board.

'Ava,' said Mrs Cook. 'Where are your glasses today?'
Ava looked down at her schoolbag.
She hated her glasses.

Mrs Cook picked up a large book
and opened it in front of Ava.

'If only Little Red Riding Hood had put on her glasses the day she went to visit her grandmother!' said Mrs Cook.

'She would have seen the big teeth and big eyes.'
Ava stopped crying. Mrs Cook turned the pages.

'Imagine if Hansel and Gretel had worn their
glasses when they got lost in the woods.
They would have seen the signs pointing
them safely home.'

Ava looked brighter.

'Everybody knows Humpty Dumpty's sad story, but if he had put on his specs, he would never have fallen off that wall.'

Ava nodded and added, 'If the king's horses and king's men had worn their glasses, they would have been able to put him back together again!'

'And have you heard of Little Bo-Peep who lost her sheep?'

'She never lost them at all! With glasses, she would have seen those woolly faces all around her.'

'And if little Miss Muffet had been wearing her glasses,

she would have seen that big spider and used her flyspray!'

Ava reached into her schoolbag and
pulled out her glasses.

The letters written on the board became clear,
and the words made sense. Ava could understand
whole sentences!

She smiled and began to read.